"I won't hurt you, Emily," Cloud murmured.

"There are many ways to hurt a person, Mr. Ryder," she retorted softly. She trembled as he removed her bodice. "You think it will not pain me to play the whore for you?"

Tugging off her shoes and stockings, he studied her flushed face. "Not the whore, Emily. My lover."

"How so? Do I not buy your help and protection with my body?"

"Women have sold their bodies for far less." He tipped up her chin and made her face him. "I haven't even had you yet, but I know you're no whore. Now no more talk."

She had no choice but to obey him, for his mouth hungrily covered hers. Emily was so caught up in the sensations that his kisses produced that she was only vaguely aware of his skillful removal of her clothes . . .

Books by Hannah Howell

ONLY FOR YOU * MY VALIANT KNIGHT
UNCONQUERED * WILD ROSES
A TASTE OF FIRE * HIGHLAND DESTINY
HIGHLAND HONOR * HIGHLAND
PROMISE * A STOCKINGFUL OF JOY
HIGHLAND VOW * HIGHLAND KNIGHT
HIGHLAND HEARTS * HIGHLAND BRIDE
HIGHLAND ANGEL * HIGHLAND
GROOM * HIGHLAND WARRIOR
RECKLESS * HIGHLAND CONQUEROR
HIGHLAND CHAMPION * HIGHLAND
LOVER * HIGHLAND VAMPIRE
THE ETERNAL HIGHLANDER * MY
IMMORTAL HIGHLANDER
CONQUEROR'S KISS * HIGHLAND
BARBARIAN * BEAUTY AND THE BEAST
HIGHLAND SAVAGE * HIGHLAND
THIRST * HIGHLAND WEDDING
HIGHLAND WOLF * SILVER FLAME
HIGHLAND FIRE * NATURE OF THE
BEAST * HIGHLAND CAPTIVE
HIGHLAND SINNER * MY LADY CAPTOR
IF HE'S WICKED * WILD CONQUEST
IF HE'S SINFUL * KENTUCKY BRIDE *
IF HE'S WILD * YOURS FOR ETERNITY
COMPROMISED HEARTS

Published by Kensington Publishing
Corporation

HANNAH HOWELL

COMPROMISED HEARTS

ZEBRA BOOKS
KENSINGTON PUBLISHING CORP.
http://www.kensingtonbooks.com

ZEBRA BOOKS are published by

Kensington Publishing Corp.
119 West 40th Street
New York, NY 10018

All Kensington titles, imprints, and distributed lines
are available at special quantity discounts for bulk pur-
chases for sales promotion, premiums, fund-raising,
educational, or institutional use.

Special book excerpts or customized printings can
also be created to fit specific needs. For details, write
or phone the office of the Kensington Special Sales
Manager: Attn. Special Sales Department. Kensington
Publishing Corp., 119 West 40th Street, New York, NY
10018. Phone: 1-800-221-2647.

Zebra and the Z logo Reg. U.S. Pat. & TM Off.

ISBN-13: 978-1-4201-0467-7
ISBN-10: 1-4201-0467-5

First Zebra Books Printing: November 2010

Previously published by Leisure Books.

10   9   8   7   6   5   4   3   2   1

Printed in the United States of America

She had already walked for two days but had yet to see any sign of civilization. She could not believe that the territory could be quite so empty. Then again, the Indians could well have something to do with the emptiness.

A shudder rippled through her. The memory of the slaughter was still too clear. Those poor farmers had not deserved such a death. They had never harmed anyone. The Indians were extracting their revenge from the wrong people.

Emily's penchant for cleaniness had been all that had saved her. She had noticed a small creek, and had walked some distance from camp for a bath. It had not been far enough away, however, to spare her from hearing the sounds of the massacre. She wondered if the war whoops, shots, and screams would ever fade from her memory or cease to haunt her dreams.

Returning to the smoldering wagons had been the most difficult thing she'd ever done. The smell of death still tainted her nostrils. The Indians had spared neither man nor woman. The only survivor was a child.

It would always puzzle her. There seemed no reason for three-year-old Thornton Sears' survival. He had been walking amongst the dead. She could only assume that he had been hidden and had stayed so until the danger was past. His plump little body was unhurt, his thick brown curls still intact, and his green eyes unclouded by a horror he was

2

probably too young to fully understand. He was alive and she prayed she could keep him that way.

The dirt on her hands from her fall began to sting her blisters. She really should not have lingered to bury the dead, although she doubted that the two days lost to that gruesome chore would make any difference in the end. During that time she had meticulously combed through the ruins, salvaging one extremely recalcitrant mule, a rickety cart, a few belongings of hers and Thornton's and a pitiful supply of food and water. She was carefully rationing what she had, but she feared that it was not enough.

"Go home now?"

"I'm trying, darling, but I fear it is a very long way."

Emily felt like weeping but refused to give in to that weakness. She wondered what madness had caused her to leave her Boston home, then grimaced as she recalled her reasons. At the time she had received her brother's request to come live with him, perhaps teach school in the budding town of Lockridge, she had thought it was the answer to all her prayers.

She had thought that anything would be better than the life she led in her sister Carolynn's home. She didn't know which was worse—caring for Carolynn's three spoiled children or trying to elude Carolynn's husband. At times the man had seemed possessed of a score of hands, all trying to grab her. There had been no help from her sister. Caro thought her children were living saints, and she clearly hoped that her sister would take Caro's place under her husband, thus relieving Caro of one wifely duty she plainly found repulsive.

Used to a life that had never been ideal, Emily had suffered stoically. Born late to Charles and Mary Brockinger, she had had little sense of family. All her siblings had been full grown, while she was an infant. It hurt to remember it, but her parents had made it abundantly clear that she was an unwanted surprise. Only Harper, she thought with a soft smile, had loved her but he had left to find his own life when she was only ten.

She touched the pocket where Harper's letter rested. She had wasted no time in answering it. Although she had not seen Harper for eight years, his smile had always lingered in her mind as one of the few bright spots in her life. Without hesitation she had set out for Colorado.

She just wished Harper had sent some money. Carolynn had adamantly refused to let go of a single penny of her plentiful horde, so Emily had been forced to take the long, hard, dangerous route to Colorado. Until now she had not really minded that. Thirst, dust, hunger, heat, and all the hardships of travel across the country by wagon train had not deterred her. The savage deaths she had witnessed were another matter. She was no coward, but she was, after all, only a girl of nineteen who had never been outside of Boston.

Her feet hurt, her sensible shoes long since worn out from the rough terrain. Carrying Thornton was easier than letting him walk, safer than setting him on the already heavily laden mule, but her back and shoulders were now screaming out for relief. The stubborn mule added to her problems, for she often had to drag him along, and the rope had left its painful mark upon her tender palms.

Worse, she decided, was the fear she could not shake. It seeped through her veins like poison. She had little idea of where she was headed, only knowing that it was west, and that she was alone and unarmed in a territory filled with Indians. She could only keep walking, however, and hope that the Indians were far too busy to bother with one woman, one child and one very cantankerous mule.

She met the day's end with little emotion. All she could be glad of was that she and Thornton still lived.

As she set up a small campfire, her gaze settled upon Thornton who sat quietly playing with some pebbles. Protected by his extreme youth, he had accepted his family's loss quickly. He had only cried a little as the beginning, then switched his dependence and affection to her. Dishing out his share of the oatmeal, Emily prayed that she would not fail him. The responsibility weighed heavily upon her.

When they curled up beneath the cart to sleep, she was glad of the warmth of his sturdy little body. He was too small to be any real help but he made her feel less alone. Although she knew she ought to stay awake to keep watch, she soon fell asleep. Emily sadly admitted to herself, as she welcomed oblivion, that she had no defense against the Indians, so keeping watch seemed a fruitless exercise.

Cloud decided that nothing was more frustrating than trying to talk the major out of his plans. Newly arrived from a military school, the man had no concept of how to fight the Indians. Cloud could only hope that the man would learn his lessons without killing himself or too many of his men. He, however, had no intention of waiting around to watch.

"Off again?" drawled James Carlin as he leaned against the hitching post.

Cloud did not look up from saddling his roan stallion. "Don't think I'll be back this time."

"Not even for sweet Abigail? It's a hard man you are, Cloud Ryder."

Looking quickly in the direction of James's nod, Cloud grimaced. He had hoped to leave without a scene, but by the look on Abby's face he knew that was now impossible. Despite her skill in bed, he was as anxious to leave her as he was to escape the young major's inevitable folly. Abigail was far too possessive, expecting of him more than he had ever offered. It had been a mistake to get involved with her.

"Sweet Abigail is reason enough to leave—fast," he muttered. "She wants to lock me up tighter than an old maid's corset." He did not share in James's soft laughter.

James studied Cloud briefly. The man's attraction for women was a puzzle to him. A scar cut Cloud's lean features, giving his carved face an intimidating fierceness that had caused many a man to back off. Although only one quarter Cherokee, Cloud often looked more savage then some full-blooded Indian. James could only wonder if the man's aloofness was what drew women.

"You didn't tell me you were leaving," Abigail said tightly as she reached Cloud's side.

"No? Must've slipped my mind," Cloud drawled as he turned to look at the well-formed brunette.

Abigail drew her breath in. She was sorely tempted to scratch out his eyes. Yet despite her anger, her blood ran hot as she looked at his tall, lean body. She hated him for that. He had toyed with her but, worse, she had lost the game.

"How can you be so cool after what we've shared?" She found it surprisingly easy to bring tears to her eyes.

"Honey, you were no blushing virgin and I sure as hell didn't teach you the tricks you knew," he said cruelly. "Don't play the offended maid. The role doesn't suit you."

"You bastard," she hissed. "You've made it plain to the whole fort that you spent your nights with me. Now that they all know you've used me for your whore, and you're just going to up and leave me?"

"Yup." He took her slap without flinching, but caught her wrist when she prepared to strike him a second time. "I wouldn't if I were you."

The chill in his voice made her shiver. With what few scraps of dignity she could muster, she left him. Cloud turned back to his preparations for leaving.

"One of these days you're going to be shot by one of the women you treat so coldly."

"No doubt. Don't waste any of your sympathy on Abigail. She knows more tricks than a rich man's mistress. She'll recover and probably trap some poor fool into marrying her. I made her no promises. I break none by leaving her. She played the game well, but she's a sore loser."

For a moment James said nothing, but then he asked, "Am I wrong in thinking you really won't come back?"

"Said so, didn't I?"

"Said it before too, but you always came back."

"Not this time. After the war I meant to settle. I thought I'd had enough of drifting and fighting. I was wrong. I was still itchy. Well, the itch is gone."

"I find that hard to believe."

"Why? A man's got to settle sometime."

"Just can't see it with you. You got too much restlessness in you."

Cloud shrugged. "Maybe. Still, it ain't being satisfied with roaming and fighting."

"What do you intend to do?"

"Go back to my land and finally do something with it. Wolfe must be damned tired of keeping an eye on it. He's got his own piece to look after."

"Where is your land? You've described it but never said exactly where it is."

"The San Luis Valley. If I leave now I can make it over the mountains before the snow blocks the pass. Come spring I'll start making my spread something more than a patch of grass. Maybe I'll even have a house by the time the Ryder clan gathers." He mounted his horse and held his hand out to James. "Take care. Don't go with that fool if you can help it. He'll get you killed for sure. Damn fool's got his head in the mud."

"It'll take more than that young shavetail's ignorance to kill me." James clasped Cloud's hand. "Take care yourself. Hope you find what you're searching for."

"Never know. Look me up if you get down San Luis Valley way."

He rode out of the fort without a backward glance. It was the end of yet another chapter in his life. He was tired of killing and destruction. Finally he was ready to stay in one place and put down roots. Maybe he would also find some peace.

That made him laugh, a harsh noise that grated on his ears. James was right. He was searching for something, but he could not say what. No matter what he did, who he met or how many miles he covered, there lingered an emptiness within him. There was a strange hunger in him that no amount of food or water could satisfy.

Cursing softly, he turned his mount southwest. It was a long way to his ranch-to-be, and he refused to spend the time worrying over something so intangible. There were enough natural and very tangible things to concern him. Distraction was something that could easily proved fatal.

When he first saw the woman as he crested a knoll, he thought her a figment of his imagination. A woman strolling through the plains with a fashionable bonnet on her head and a parasol in hand? It was a sight too ludicrous to be real, yet he could not deny the evidence of his eyes.

Riding a little closer yet staying out of her direct line of sight, he realized that the strange hump on her back was a child. Shaking his head in disbelief, he began to follow her.

As he watched her fall and pick herself up a third time, he began to laugh softly even while he admired her persistence. She was so plainly out of her element that it was funny. So was the sight of her strolling through hostile Indian territory as if she were taking a promenade in the park. The only thing that kept him from laughing was the grim reality of danger all around.

"The silly bitch can be seen for miles, Savannah," he muttered to his horse. "Maybe it's true that God watches out for fools, drunkards, and children. Got us two of the three just ahead. Where's her man?"

Fascinated, he followed her as she cursed the land she stumbled over and threatened the mule with prolonged and painful retribution. Try as he would, Cloud could not figure out how she had arrived in the middle of nowhere with her child strapped to her back like some papoose. Her clothes, although tattered and dusty, still retained their fashionable air, telling him that she was no die-hard pioneer woman.

He settled himself on a knoll overlooking her campsite when she paused for the night. His reluctance either to show himself or leave her puzzled him, but he did not fight it. It had been a long time since he had been so thoroughly entertained.

It was not until the child was settled and asleep that she let her weariness show. Even from a distance, Cloud could tell how hard she fought giving in to tears.

He tensed slightly when she knelt before the fire and removed her bodice, using a little of the precious water to clean off the dust that clung to her. When she removed her camisole, he shifted restlessly, his eyes fixed hungrily upon the full pale breasts as she washed. By the time she had finished her bathing, he was aching. Then, as if to further taunt her unseen audience, she undid her hair.

"My God," he breathed, "the Indians would kill each other for a scalp like that."

By the light of the fire and the moon, her hair shone white. It fell in long thick waves to her slim hips. Cloud wanted to bury himself in it; his palms itched to run through its heavy length as her brush was doing. He did not think he had ever seen anything so beautiful nor so desirable despite the wide range of women he had known.

After she had lain down with the child he sat watching her for a while longer. He needed time to quell his desire before he got any closer to the woman.

Deeming himself once more in control, he decided to go down to her campsite. There was little point in setting up one of his own when hers was so close. He also wanted to dampen the fire, which might draw attention to the woman.

The mule eyed him warily as he tied Savannah to a bush, but it made no noise. After securing his pack horse and relieving the animal of its burden, he turned his attention to the sleeping pair under the cart. He was curious to see if the woman's face was as lovely as the rest of her.

Pausing only to douse the fire, he sat down near the cart. The woman and the child slept on, unaware of him. Cloud shook his head. They were both babes in the wood, defenseless and ignorant.

Studying her face, he realized that she was very young. In fact, she hardly looked old enough to have borne the child tucked up against her. Cloud decided the boy must take after his father, for he lacked his mother's delicacy of looks and her fairness of coloring.

Her skin cried out to be touched, its light honey-colored expanse looking as soft and smooth as silk. Faintly arched brows, several shades darker than her brilliant hair, furrowed occasionally as her dreams grew more troubled. The lashes that lay in thick arcs on her cheeks were also dark and naturally curly. A full ripe mouth was slightly parted as she slept, partially revealing straight white teeth. Her nose was the only less than perfect feature in her small oval face. It ran small and straight to the tip then suddenly turned up ever so slightly, disrupting an otherwise classical perfection.

She had left off her bodice, having rinsed it in the water that she then gave the mule, and hung it on the bush to dry. His eyes fixed upon the smooth swell of her breasts above the lacy camisole and he nearly groaned. The desire had been controlled but not vanquished.

Stretching out, he leaned against the cart wheel, placing his rifle across his lap. There would be little sleep for him until he was out of the area troubled by Indians. Senses well-honed by the war allowed him to doze yet be alert to danger. He almost wished he could sleep as blissfully as the pair beneath the cart, but he knew too well how dangerous that could be.

A sound from the young woman drew his gaze back to her and he realized that she was having a nightmare. She muttered fretfully and tears oozed from beneath her eyelids as she relived some horror in her dreams. Her restlessness caused the boy to whimper in his sleep.

"Hush, sweetheart," he murmured as he smoothed his hand over her brow in a soothing caress.

"Harper?" she cried softly even as she settled down.

"Ssssh. There's nothing here to trouble you. Go to sleep, little lady."

After the pair had again settled, Cloud returned to his half-sleep, half-vigil. He wondered who Harper was and decided he was her husband. Frowning, he searched the long fingers of her small delicate hands but saw no ring. Either she had no husband or he was dead. Either way suited Cloud. He fully intended to satisfy the desire she stirred in him and a husband would only complicate matters. A small child was complication enough.

She stretched and turned, disturbing the light blanket that covered her. A smile touched his harsh features as he glimpsed her feet. They were as small and delicate as the rest of her. His smile faded quickly when he saw how her feet had suffered from the walking she had done. He was surprised she had stayed on her feet at all. Every step must have pained her, yet she had struggled on.

"Stubborn as your mule," he muttered as he reached to tuck the blanket around her feet.

He paused, his gaze drifting up the length of slender leg exposed by her bunched-up petticoats. He moved his hand over her calf and up to where her petticoats rested high up on her silken thighs. She moved and made a soft noise that brought a satisfied smile to his face as he finally tucked the blanket back in place.

Experience told him how to read those small signs. Even in her sleep she had warmed to his touch. There was passion in her. Cloud knew it would be good and found it hard to resist the temptation to slip beneath the blanket with her immediately. Waiting would be hard, but he did not plan to wait long.

The night passed slowly. Twice more Cloud had to soothe the young woman's troubled sleep. That she was so evidently filled with fear made her dogged progress all the more remarkable. She plainly had the strength to subdue those fears when she was awake, forcing herself to continue despite them.

When dawn lightened the sky, he washed himself and watered the mounts. He then set about relighting the small fire and preparing a breakfast of sorts. As he had hoped, the smell of coffee began to wake the sleepers.

The boy woke first, studying Cloud for a long moment before rising. With the uncanny sixth sense a child so often has, the boy sensed that he was no threat. Keeping a shy watch on him, however, the boy went to relieve himself then came to squat by him near the fire.

"Mornin'," he said finally. "I'm Thornton."

"I'm Cloud Ryder. Hungry?" He dished out some oatmeal for the boy when he nodded.

"This is good as Mama's."

"Have you and your mama walked far?"

"Miles and miles. We're going home. 'Way from Injuns."

"Where's your pa?" Cloud sipped his coffee, occasionally glancing towards the still sleeping girl.

"Wiv the angels," Thornton said calmly, repeating Emily's explanation. "Injuns kilt him dead so the angels took him. They take dead folk, you know."

Cloud nodded even as he mused that the angels would no doubt toss *him* back. He had become too hard and too many men had died at his hands. He would probably never see Heaven's gates. And though the killing had been part of a war, he doubted that fact would save his soul.

"You and your mama are alone then?" he prompted and the boy nodded.

To Thornton, Emily was his mother. The

angels had taken his other mother and left him a new one. He was blissfully ignorant of any misconception the man opposite him was forming.

"Are you going home too?" the boy asked.

"Yup. Going to set up my ranch."

"Wiv cows?" Cloud nodded. "I fink my new home has cows."

"Where is your new home?"

"Out dere." Thornton pointed towards the faintly visible mountains. "Sandly's, I fink."

Smiling, Cloud gave up trying to get any specifics. Children of Thornton's age were not very concerned with details.

"I fink Mama's getting awake."

"Mmmm, I think you're right."

Watching her stretch made Cloud's loins tighten. Despite her delicate build, there was an unconscious voluptuousness to her movements. He could not wait to feel her beneath him, her lithe grace working to satisfy him.

She sat up, rubbing her eyes in a distinctly childlike gesture. When her gaze fell on the spot where Thornton had lain he saw her tense. An instant later he found himself staring appreciatively into a pair of wide, somewhat frantic jade green eyes.

Chapter Two

After assuring herself that Thornton was alive, Emily stared at the man crouched by the fire. Her relief over Thornton's safety rapidly vanished, and she wished desperately that she had some weapon.

When the stranger stood up, she trembled. The man was well over six feet tall. Although he was lean, she was not deceived into thinking him lacking in strength. A woman who could stretch to two inches over five feet if she wore shoes and stood on tiptoe had no chance against him.

Thick hair, the blue-black of a raven's wing, hung to his broad shoulders; a red bandana tied around his wide forehead and knotted at the side kept it out of his eyes. A buckskin shirt hugged his muscular torso and was partly unlaced to reveal a smooth, dark chest. Dark pants disappeared into buckskin boots that hugged the bottom half of his long muscular legs.

As if his height and strength were not intimidating enough, there were the harsh lines of his face. High cheekbones and a high-bridged nose told of his Indian blood, as did the coppery tint of his dark complexion. His thin-lipped mouth was set in an unreadable straight line. The scar added a fierceness to his lean features that did nothing to ease Emily's fears.

Swallowing her panic, she met his gaze. His eyes were a deep, rich brown ringed with amber. She had never seen such eyes. Neither had she seen eyes so lacking in expression.

"Please," she said softly, "don't hurt the boy."

Cloud shook himself. He realized that she thought him an Indian and, quite naturally, had assumed the worst. He had known the harsh sting of prejudice all too often in the past.

" 'Bout time you woke up, ma'am. Day's near gone."

She closed her eyes briefly in relief. "You aren't an Indian."

"Well, partly. Grandmother on my father's side was Cherokee. Coffee's made."

Following the direction of his gaze, she recalled her state of undress and blushed. "If you will give me but a moment's privacy so that I might dress?"

"Reckon so," he drawled, but took his time turning around and returning to the campfire.

After dressing and making a hasty trip to some nearby bushes, Emily tentatively approached the fire. She was not foolish enough to think herself safe simply because the man was not an Indian. From the time she had changed from a child into a woman she had known that even the most innocent-appearing of men could prove dangerous. Out here in the middle of nowhere, the danger was that much greater.

"What's your name?" he asked, ignoring her wariness as he served her coffee.

"Emily," she replied softly as she sat down next to Thornton.

"Emily what?" he demanded.

"Emily Cordelia Mason Brockinger," she recited a little tartly. "And you, sir?"

Biting back a grin, he replied, "Cloud Ryder."

She blinked. "I beg your pardon?"

"Cloud Ryder. R-y-d-e-r. Just what are you doing out here?"

"Besides walking?" she retorted dryly and saw his lips twitch. "We're headed for the mountains."

" 'The mountains' is a little vague."

"The San Luis Valley." She frowned when he laughed softly. "That's funny?"

"Actually, I was thinking of what Thornton

21

answered when I asked him the same question. He said 'Sandly's.' " He felt a tremor low in his belly when he heard her soft, husky laugh. "You're going the wrong way," he said.

"Nonsense," she said in her best schoolmarm voice. "I am headed west."

"Fair enough, but the valley's also south by several weeks' ride."

Her heart sank. If it was several weeks' ride, then it was many weeks' walking. Somehow she had let herself believe that, if she reached the mountains, she would be fine. To hear that she would still have to travel many weeks southward was almost devastating. It was a struggle not to weep, but stiff Yankee pride kept her from showing any weakness before a stranger.

Cloud covertly watched her struggle. The way she put her small chin up amused him even while he felt a twinge of admiration. He had seen how the news had devastated her, but she was not going to let it break her. She had a strength of character he could only approve of.

"I see. So I am not even half the way there yet."

"Depends on where you started from."

"Boston originally, but I started walking two days ago."

"Why?"

"The Indians attacked the wagon train I was with. They killed everyone."

He heard the touch of lingering horror in

her voice and knew that was the incident that darkened her dreams. "Why not you or Thornton?"

"I was away from the campsite. I'm not quite sure how Thornton survived. He hasn't really said."

"Papa put me in a hole," Thornton said suddenly. "He told me stay put 'till all's quiet and I did."

Emily barely checked her tears. The loss of so many friends was still too fresh. She thought of how eager the young Sears couple had been, how full of plans.

"I'm sorry, ma'am," Cloud said quietly. "How many were there?"

"Nearly twenty." She gazed at her hands, still blistered from the chore of burying so many.

"So you picked up your boy and started walking west?"

"Two days later, yes."

"Why'd you wait?"

"The burying took me two whole days."

"You buried everyone?" he said softly.

She read his reaction as one of surprise. "Well, I did not dig twenty graves. I didn't think they would mind if I put a child in with his mother or father or put loved ones together." She shivered at the memory.

"That was a damned stupid thing to do," he snapped, glaring at her.

Emily decided that she preferred a lack of expression in his eyes to the hard, cold anger that now lit them. "It was the Christian thing to do, sir."

"Christian be damned. It was a fool thing to do."

"What was I to do?" she snapped, growing angry herself. "Leave them for the carrion?"

"Damn right." His attitude was not softened by her shock. "Listen, you fool woman, what do you think's going to occur to those Indians if they return to that site?"

"Why should they? They cannot do any more."

"Maybe they'll just pass it on their way to someplace else. How the hell should I know? The point is that they'll see those graves and know somebody survived."

She felt the color leave her cheeks. "That will matter to them?"

"Damn right it'll matter. It'll set them looking for you. They don't know it was only a fool woman and a babe. They don't want to leave survivors, girl—not in the mood they're in now."

Taking a deep breath to settle the fears he was stirring up, she said, "I had to bury them."

"Tell that to the Indians. They could be hot after you even now. Not that you'd see them coming."

Although she knew full well that she was almost totally incompetent out here on the plains, she resented his attitude. He could take into consideration the fact that she was a city girl from the east, not a cowboy, and give her some credit for what she had accomplished. Instead, he spoke to her as if she were severely lacking in brains and good sense. She simmered with fury as he lectured her.

"Marching across the plains as if you're on some Sunday stroll. You stick out like a sore thumb. I'm surprised you haven't lost that hair already."

"What am I supposed to do? Crawl to the mountains on my stomach?"

"Might be a damn good idea."

"Stop cursing."

"Look, you little idiot, you haven't got the sense God gave a goose. You parade across hostile country without even trying to keep out of sight, then strip down afore a blazing fire for all to see."

"You watched me?" she gasped, color flooding her face.

"Damn right. Show was free."

He caught her wrist when she swung at him and tugged her towards him. Emily sprawled on his lap, staring up into his harsh face. She tried only once to sit up, found herself held firmly, and did not try again. Struggling against a man of his strength and size would only get her hurt.

Cloud studied the woman glaring up at him. Her full breasts rose and fell rapidly with the force of her anger. The thick silvery hair he so admired lay like a blanket over his legs. He gave into temptation and buried one hand in its heavy waves, finding it soft as silk.

"I followed you for hours, woman. You never took notice of me, kept no watch for trouble."

"And just what would you suggest I do if I saw trouble coming?" she asked tartly.

"How about running for your life? Or the boy's? Oh no, you set your pretty eyes on the mountains and trudge straight ahead with all the blind, stupid doggedness of your damned mule. You just ain't thinking, girl."

"I will keep your criticism in mind," she said coolly. "Now, would you release me, please?"

"Not just yet," he drawled, tightening his grip on her hair and urging her face toward his.

Emily's experience with men consisted of an occasional unwanted embrace resulting in a slap or, if the swain was too ardent, a well-placed knee. She knew the danger signals, however, and could sense when a man's thoughts turned carnal. Cloud Ryder's had definitely turned that way. She tensed, but his grip on her hair forced her to obey his urging.

"Let me go," she demanded coldly.

"Not just yet," he murmured against her mouth.

She tried to keep her lips closed, but the moment his mouth covered hers, she knew that would be far from easy. Despite the hard line of his mouth, his lips were warm and soft. She felt her own mouth soften beneath his as a strange heat began to spread through her body. That frightened her far more than the fact that this stranger was taking a kiss that had not been offered.

When he forced his tongue through the weakened barriers of her lips she felt that warmth begin to curl through her body. She tried to break free of his hold but failed. A moment later she succumbed to the probing intoxication of his tongue.

What pulled her back to her senses was the way her mouth followed his when it began to pull away. Her eyes widened with shock at her own actions. She abruptly broke free of his hold, and with little grace and a great deal of haste scrambled back to her original place next to a wide-eyed Thornton.

A slow smile creased his face as Cloud poured himself another cup of coffee, his gaze on her flushed face. She was a warm one, her warmth not dimmed at all by the recent death of her man. Despite her resistance, he had sensed the quick build of her passion. She would undoubtedly have a store of excuses and evasions, so he began to plot a way to get her back into his arms in the shortest time possible.

His smile annoyed her, so Emily ignored it. What she found hard to ignore was the way his eyes narrowed slightly as he watched her. She wished she knew what was going on behind those eyes. Something told her that it did not bode well for her.

"We gonna get walking again?" asked Thornton.

"Yes. We cannot waste a day." She rose to begin collecting their belongings.

"Don't forget your parasol." Cloud nodded towards that item. "No stroll is complete without one."

"Don't you have somewhere to go?" she asked icily.

"Matter of fact, I do." He stood up. "The San Luis Valley. Got a ranch there."

Emily gaped after him as he strode over to his horses.

"Are you really going to the San Luis Valley?"

"Just said so, didn't I?" He did not pause in his preparations.

"Then Thornton and I can come along with you."

"Nope."

She stared at him in open-mouthed disbelief. It had taken a lot to ask him; it had in fact been an act of sheer desperation. Emily could not believe he would refuse to help her and Thornton.

"You would leave us behind? All on our own?"

"Yup." He turned to look at her, schooling his face to remain impassive. She must never guess that he was bluffing. "You're a walking disaster, honey. I sure as hell don't need the kind of trouble you could bring me. I'd like to reach my land alive. In fact, I intend to."

"How can you be so heartless? You have made it abundantly plain that you think me

28

totally incompetent. Leaving us on our own
is tantamount to murder."

He shrugged and began to saddle Savannah. "Got my own scalp to think about."

"I can pay you," she blurted out after a
moment of frantic thought.

"You've got money?"

"Well, not exactly. I have a few things that
can be traded for cash," she added hastily
as he began to mount. "A few pieces of
jewelry."

"How much will they bring?" he asked
coolly, turning to face her again.

"Fifty, perhaps a hundred dollars."

"Not worth risking my life for." Again he
started to mount.

"It's all I have," she said weakly, seeing her
last chance slip away.

"Maybe." He turned and slowly approached her. "Maybe not."

She wondered if she had been foolish to
let him know that she had collateral of any
sort. He could easily take it and still leave
her and Thornton stranded. The man certainly had not acted the gentleman. She could not
help fearing that she had made yet another
very large mistake.

"I could perhaps get more when we reach
San Luis Valley."

"From Harper?" he asked quietly, coming
to a halt but inches from her.

"Harper? How do you know Harper?" She
refused to allow him to intimidate her into
stepping back.

"You said his name while you slept."

"Oh. Well, I'm sure Harper could add some. He would be glad that I had reached him safe and sound."

"I'm sure he would be. I don't want anything from Harper."

His deep, smooth voice was doing strange things to her insides and she frowned. "What do you want, then? If you would state a price, I could say yes or no."

"You," he stated flatly as he took hold of a lock of her hair, caressing it between his long fingers.

"What?" she croaked, sure she had misunderstood him.

"I want you," he purred, moving his hand so that it cupped the side of her slim neck where her pulse throbbed frantically.

"Did we not just fight a war to put an end to slavery?"

"Won it, too. Not slavery, darling, but service. You accommodate me and I'll accommodate you."

"I cannot believe you would take advantage of my desperate situation."

"Believe it. I'm not overly endowed with scruples when it comes to getting what I want."

"How true. The milk of human kindness plainly started to curdle once I crossed the Ohio."

"No doubt. Well, do we have a deal?"

"No, sir." She stepped back, away from his touch. "We do not. If I were inclined to play the whore, I would have done it back in Boston."

He shrugged and turned back to his horses. Cloud was not convinced that he had lost his gamble yet. There was time for her to rethink her refusal. Once she was sure that he really would leave her and the boy, she would change her mind.

Nonetheless, he began to plot a second course of action, in case he was wrong. Even he was not callous enough to leave her and the boy on their own. There was something about her that made him feel unusually protective.

Emily stood like a rock, her mind not functioning for a moment. The men she had known had not all been gentlemen, but she was sure none of them would have threatened to leave her and a small boy alone in a hostile wilderness. She could not believe the stranger really meant to do so.

"We going home now?" Thornton asked as he ambled up to her and took her hand in his.

Emily looked down at the child. His green eyes were filled with trust and hope. He believed her capable of keeping them alive, of knowing what to do and how to get them to safety. Unfortunately, his trust was misplaced.

She knew nothing of the country they walked through or the dangers it held. Emily knew the stranger was right—she was stumbling on with all the blind, stupid doggedness of her irascible mule.

She found herself asking if her chastity was all that precious. It might be worth protecting with her own life, but was it worth Thornton's as well? The boy certainly could not understand the concept of honor or chastity.

"Sir?" she croaked, taking a hesitant step toward the horse and rider. "Sir?" she called in a stronger voice as she realized she had no choice but to accept his terms. "Mr. Ryder?"

He finally stopped, turning in his saddle to look at her. Although he had heard her the first time, he had ignored the faint cry. It could have been a false alarm. The way she stood there with her little chin raised told him she had made a decision. He only hoped it was the one he wanted.

She gently eased her hand free of Thornton's clasp and approached him. She thought resignedly that she ought to be glad that he was young, strong and attractive. Her rescuer could have been a lot less appealing; he could have taken what he wanted by force.

"Perhaps if we could discuss the terms," she began.

Dismounting, he pushed his hat back on his head and yanked her into his arms. He was amazed at how good she felt there. Cloud had held women that filled his arms better than this little Boston lady, but, oddly enough, he could not recall them now. All he could picture in his mind was how those soft curves looked without clothes.

"The terms are that we share a blanket from here to the valley."

"I am not able to make any conditions?" she squeaked as he picked her up so that their faces were level. "You ask me to concede a great deal."

"But you'll gain a great deal—your life and the boy's safety. I don't think you'll find it too hard to take."

The kiss that followed confirmed his words. Emily had always been taught that a good woman did not enjoy such attentions, and under the present circumstances, she should be repulsed. But by the time he released her mouth, she could not deny her growing eagerness. It appalled her.

She could not help wondering if that earlier kiss had influenced her decision. A little voice whispered to her that while she was saving Thornton's life and her own, she could be paying a price far higher than her chastity. She fought to quell a sudden panic. There really was no choice.

"There must be one condition," she gasped, putting her hands on his chest and pushing against him.

Cloud found it hard to halt his lovemaking. He knew he was very close to tossing her down on the ground and taking her there and then. The strength of his desire for her surprised and somewhat alarmed him, but he had no intention of turning away from her.

"And what is that condition?" he asked

tautly as he fought to control his passion.

"Consideration for the child. He must be kept as unaware as possible."

"You'll be in my arms every night. That'll be hard to hide from him."

It was impossible to keep down the blush that stained her face, but she struggled to ignore it. "I understand that, but surely there is no need to be too blatant."

"In other words, don't carry on when the boy's standing there staring at us."

Seeing him looking over her shoulder she followed the direction of his gaze. Thornton was watching them with intense curiosity. "That says it quite nicely, Mr. Ryder."

Carefully, and with a reluctance he could not hide, he set her on her feet before him. "I think I can manage that. So?" He brushed his knuckles over her cheek. "A deal?"

Swallowing her pride, she nodded. "A deal."

She thought his smile was annoying. He had gotten what he wanted. There was no need to gloat. Shooting him a glare, she went to pack up her things.

Cloud returned to the small campsite. Whatever guilt he felt about using her desperate situation to suit his own needs was easily vanquished. He found that, in this case, he had very few scruples. He would get her any way he could.

"This horse is too fine for a pack animal anyhow," he said as he removed his things from the animal's back and stowed them in the cart. "She'll serve better as a mount for you. Of course, you'll have to ride astride."

Emily bit her lip as she watched him prepare the horse for her. She had no fear of horses, but she had no experience riding. It was difficult to admit to him that she had never ridden a horse. However, she knew she had to speak up. She doubted she could pretend that she knew what she was doing and he ought to know her limitations. Emily simply wished that she did not have quite so many of them.

"Excuse me," she ventured timidly as he stowed the last of his things in the cart.

"Mmmmm?"

"Well, I think you had better look at me. It's that sort of news."

Frowning, he turned to face her. "You'd better put that hair up."

"Pardon?" Her hand went to her still unbound hair. "Oh. Of course."

"Indian sees that lot and he'll be after you like a fox after a chicken."

"I see, but I must inform you of something. It could be important."

"Get on with it then."

"I cannot ride a horse," she said weakly.

"Not at all?"

"I've never been on the back of one in my whole life."

"How the hell did you get around?"

"I walked or went by carriage."

Muttering things she was glad she did not understand, he placed Thornton on his horse,

Chapter Three

Emily was sure there was a bruise to mark each new lesson in horsemanship. If Cloud was not cussing or yelling at her, he was laughing. Emily felt sure that she would have shot him if she'd possessed a gun.

The only good thing about riding was that it saved her feet, and the distance was certainly covered with more speed. Emily knew she would reach her destination much faster, but she was not sure she would get there alive. An immodest but judicious wrapping of her legs in her skirts had saved her from chafing but did little to cushion the jolts she suffered as she tried to learn the rhythm of her mount.

Cloud glanced at Emily and hid a grin. She

had no aptitude for riding. He doubted that she would gain much skill with time and practice either. Nevertheless, he knew she would do her utmost to keep up with him.

Fortunately, the little boy had a natural skill. Even more important, he was obedient, responding to Cloud's commands immediately. Since it looked as if he would have the boy with him for the duration of the journey, that was a blessing.

"We'll stop for the night soon," he said, glancing at the sunset.

Emily could not fully repress her sigh of relief. She prayed that there were carriages in Lockridge. After this journey, she hoped never to have to ride a horse again, even if it meant she had to walk for miles.

Nevertheless, she listened closely a short while later when Cloud instructed her in the care of her mount. That much she could do without difficulty.

After the animals were seen to, Cloud urged her to take advantage of a nearby creek. She set off at once, feeling no qualms about leaving the preparation of the meal in his hands. As she took the short walk to the creek she mused a little bitterly that he could probably do that better than she as well.

Taking advantage of the thick growth of bushes near the water, she shed her clothes. The water was brisk but she didn't mind. Simply washing away the sweat and dust eased her discomfort. The aches she suffered lost a great deal of their importance.

It was not until she donned her under-things, still damp from the rinsing she had given them, that she wondered if cleaning up had been a mistake. Smelling a little rank might have deterred Cloud Ryder. She grimaced as she shook that thought aside and finished dressing. The man was not about to be deterred by such a weak defense.

She knew it would be better not to think about what was to come. That however, was far easier said than done. She started back towards the camp and a fate she still faintly hoped could be avoided.

One look at Cloud's face told her that she did not have even a faint hope. Resolutely, she gave most of her attention to Thornton. It did not bother her at all that Cloud knew that she was deliberately ignoring him.

She resisted the urge to keep Thornton awake. She would not use the boy as a pawn. She tucked him into his blanket shortly after the meal, then told him a short story.

"Is the man taking us home?" Thornton asked sleepily.

"Yes, dear. He's also going to the San Luis Valley. He will take us to Harper."

"You ain't put your blanket next to me."

"No." She refused to blush. "I will sleep next to Mr. Ryder until we reach the valley. I won't be far away. Go to sleep, love."

She was glad of Thornton's youth, for it saved her from awkward questions. However, she was not glad of the speed with which the boy fell asleep. Emily busied herself with washing Thornton's clothes and spreading them out to dry; then she cleared away the remains of the meal. She was just about to start on some mending when a strong arm caught her around the waist.

"I suppose this is an improvement over being dragged off by one's hair," she said tartly, hiding her nervousness as he carried her toward the bed of blankets.

"Wouldn't treat that glorious hair so harshly."

Emily gave a soft cry when he tossed her onto the blanket, but the ground was surprisingly soft. Peeking beneath the thin blanket, she found a layer of furs. When she looked back at Cloud, she forgot her caustic remark about a man and his comforts, for he had shed all but his trousers.

His chest was broad, smoothly muscular, and dark. The only hair she could see started as a thin line at his navel then disappeared beneath his belt. She blushed and hastily avoided his eyes. She gave a nervous start when he knelt by her and began to take down her hastily pinned-up hair.

Cloud felt her shiver as he smoothed his hands over her loosened hair. "I won't hurt you, Emily."

"There are many ways to hurt a person, Mr. Ryder," she retorted softly. She trembled as he removed her bodice. "You think it will not pain me to play the whore for you?"

Tugging off her shoes and stockings, he studied her flushed face. "Not the whore,

Emily. My lover."

"How so? Do I not buy your help and protection with my body?"

"Women have sold their bodies for far
less." He tipped up her chin and made her
face him. "I haven't even had you yet, honey,
but I know you're no whore. Now, no more
talk."

She had no choice but to obey him, for his
mouth hungrily covered hers. Emily was so
caught up in the maelstrom of sensation his
kisses produced that she was only vaguely
aware of his skillful removal of her clothes.
The occasional half-conscious, muffled
noises of protest she did make were ruthlessly ignored and soon she was naked in his
arms.

Gently he pushed her back onto the furs.
She lay stunned both by his kisses and her
own embarrassment. No man had ever seen
her so and the shock to her sense of modesty
held her immobile beneath his dark gaze.

Cloud's eyes never left her as he shed the
last of his clothes. She was exquisite, lithe
and slender but with all the softness a man
could want. He did not think he had been so
eager to bury himself in a woman since he
had been a green youth.

Emily saw the last of his clothes tossed
aside and gasped. She was sure she would
be torn asunder. Although she had never
seen a man fully naked she was certain there
was a lot more of Cloud Ryder than there
ought to be. With a little moan, she closed

her eyes.

Seeing her fear, Cloud paused. Although many women had exclaimed over his attributes, he did not really believe he was any more of a man than other males. This little widow and mother was acting like some virgin. He wondered if she and her husband had only indulged in restrained fumbling beneath the bedclothes.

When he took her into his arms, their flesh meeting for the first time, they both trembled. Cloud smiled as he brushed his lips over her face. The passion was there for him to tap. He only hoped he could control his overwhelming need long enough to bring it to the surface.

"Sweet, lovely Emily," he murmured against her lips. "I swear I won't hurt you."

As he took her mouth in another drugging kiss, Emily felt rising heat burn away her fears. Shame flickered through her, for she knew she found enjoyment in his kiss, in the feel of his long, lean frame so close to her, and in the warmth of his touch.

A soft cry escaped her when he moved his mouth to her breasts. Although a small part of her cried out in denial, she buried her hands in his thick, glossy hair to hold his enticing mouth closer when his tongue began to taunt her nipples. Yet another cry escaped her, a cry of delight, as he replied to her unconscious urgings and drew the hard, aching tip of a breast deep into his greedy mouth.

Despite the blinding heat of her passion,

she jerked away from his touch when he slid his hand up her inner thigh. It was only a brief rejection of intimacy, for she soon succumbed to a fresh cascade of desire. Sensations, new and devastating, crashed over her from several sources. His mouth, his touch, and his rich deep voice all seduced her.

"God, you're already hot for me . . . warm, welcoming." He growled low in his throat as her fluttering hands shyly moved over him. "You can't keep fighting it, little lady. It's too strong."

He slowly kissed his way back to her flushed face as she felt him position his legs between hers. Emily shuddered with a feeling that was far more anticipation than fear. Being a virgin and a moral young lady, she feared and rejected what was about to happen. However, her body betrayed her. It arched against him, begging for whatever he would give her.

Cloud took her mouth in a fierce kiss just as he plunged into her, but suddenly he stiffened, stilled by shock. He did not need to feel her withdrawal, to hear her low moan, to know he had just roughly shattered a young woman's innocence. Releasing her mouth, he stared at her, noting that she had paled slightly and that her tear-bright gaze was accusing.

"You said you would not hurt me," she rasped even as she felt the stinging pain begin to recede.

"I thought you'd already had a man." He moved his hand over her body seeking to ease her tension and restore her passion. "I would've gone easier if I'd known." Feeling her grow soft and warm again, he began to feather kisses over her face. "It always hurts a woman the first time."

"That seems a strange and unfair arrangement," she murmured huskily as her passion began to build again. She felt a ripple of delight when he chuckled against her throat. "Is that all there is to it?"

"Nope." He began to move slowly and felt her tremble. "There's more, darlin'."

Emily found it suddenly difficult to talk. After a moment she did not need his guiding hands on her slim hips but matched his rhythm without urging. He positioned her legs around him and she clung to him as she felt herself dragged helplessly along.

Suddenly she panicked. Her body felt as if it were ready to hurl itself from some precipice. She tried to retreat from the edge, but he held her tight against him, murmuring nonsense that worked too soothe her sudden fear. Emily heard a strange cry even as she went under a blinding wave of sensation and realized that it came from her. She felt Cloud drive into her and held him there, her body drinking deeply of his release. The sound of her name breaking from his lips as he shuddered in her arms increased her own pleasure.

It was a while before he eased the intimacy

of their embrace. She lay still, feeling confused, then watched as he rose to fetch a cloth. A sensuous lethargy held her still and placid as he returned to the rough bed and pulled her into his arms.

"I knew it would be good," he muttered softly as he smoothed his hands through her hair. "Whose boy is Thornton? Damn well isn't yours as I'd first thought."

"Why should you think he was mine?"

"He calls you mama and, although he doesn't resemble you that much, he's got green eyes."

"Oh. Well, his name is Sears. He was the only child of the young couple I was traveling with."

"Traveling alone? To Harper?" Cloud wondered why the unseen Harper was beginning to irritate him.

"Yes. It might seem foolhardy but it was my only chance. I was living with my sister, and it was not the best of situations. I was taking care of her children, but I began to think that she wished me to take care of her husband as well. Harper's invitation seemed like the answer to my prayers."

"A new life," he said a little sarcastically.

"Perhaps not new, but at least different and, I hoped, better." She sighed, overwhelmed by shame. "Who knows what will happen now."

"Why do you say that? Because you're a fallen woman?" he drawled.

"To me, it is far from a matter of jest," she

snapped, fighting tears.

Rolling so that she was beneath him, he said, "Worried you face spinsterhood because you're not a virgin anymore? That might have been the way of it back east, but not out here. Women are scarce, darlin'. Virginity ain't all that important. A man out here wants a woman, not a saint."

Aware of his hard length and annoyed by that awareness, she said crossly, "I was not aiming to be a saint, but a sense of what's right never hurt anyone."

"Honey, this is right," he growled as he touched his lips to the increasing pulse in her throat.

"This is what I should be doing with my lawfully wedded husband, not with you." She gritted her teeth but failed to stem the warmth his touch engendered in her. "This is a sin."

"What a little puritan. Your head might tell you that"—he watched the tips of her breasts harden invitingly beneath his touch—"but your body says sin be damned. I never had a virgin before," he mused aloud as he bent his head to flick his tongue over each hard nub.

"Isn't that wonderful," she said in a sweet voice dripping with sarcasm, "I have given you a first."

"Yes, you have," he said slowly, but he was not referring to her innocence.

"You can't mean to—well, to do it again?"

she gasped as she became fully aware of his renewed arousal.

"Certainly do, ma'am. Are you sore?" he asked in sudden concern.

"Well, not really," she replied with an honesty that she could not restrain. "Should I be?"

"Might be tomorrow."

"Then perhaps you ought to restrain yourself, since I must ride that beast tomorrow."

"I'll give you an extra blanket. The only thing I restrain myself from is restraining myself."

"If everyone thought that way, the world would be in chaos."

"Thought it was." He brushed his lips over hers. "This time you'll participate."

"Not on your life."

"It's not my life at stake," he reminded her coolly.

"You are a complete bastard, Mr. Ryder," she said icily.

"So I've been told, darlin'. Now, shut up."

Much to her annoyance, she did. Worse, she did participate to some extent. Yet again they scaled passion's heights, their bodies in perfect sensual harmony. When he finally eased the embrace, the lethargy she had felt before now weighted her eyelids. She did not even have the strength to scold herself for the way she cuddled up to him.

"I must put some clothes on," she murmured sleepily.

"No, you don't." He ran his hand slowly over her side until he let it rest upon the gentle curve of her hip.

"Thornton. Mustn't let him see me. Might not wake up before him."

"Well, wear my shirt. There'll be less to take off if I want you again."

Groggily she started to don the shirt he held out for her, her gaze fixed upon him with sleepy annoyance. "Don't I have any say in the matter?"

"Our deal, you'll recall."

"I have a feeling I shan't be allowed to forget it for a moment."

"Doubt I'll have the energy to remind you that often."

She made a soft noise of disgust as she lay down. But she did not resist when he tucked her up against him spoon-fashion. It felt much too nice and she was much too tired.

Cloud felt her breathing grow soft and even with sleep. She felt good tucked up against him. He had no urge to seek a private corner to sleep in as he had so often in the past.

That puzzled him almost as much as the strength of the desire he felt for her. He could not attribute it to a lengthy celibacy, not after a week of Abigail's assiduous attentions. Neither could he claim it was due to her skill, for she had none except what came naturally. Her shy, reluctant touch had none of Abigail's practiced enticement, but it made him burn.

He decided not to think about it. It was just one of those things. As he slipped into the light sleep of the hardened soldier, he decided to just accept and enjoy.

Screams mingled with bloodthirsty war cries. Emily clasped her hands over her ears, but the sounds went on and on until she thought she would go mad. They did not even stop when the shooting did. When the silence finally came, she could still hear the echoes of the battle.

Slowly she walked toward the thin column of smoke. So much blood! She gagged over the warm, fresh stench of it. Shutting her eyes tightly did not close out the sight of so many bodies cast like stones over the ground, some twisted, some straight, but all soaked in their life's blood. Friends lay mutilated, some more than others. She ached to tear the vision from her eyes.

It was a while before her horror-gripped mind became aware of a deep, soothing voice and a calloused but gentle hand that smoothed over her forehead, driving the demons away. "Cloud?"

"Ssssh, honey. Don't let it haunt you," he murmured against her ear.

She turned in his hold, borrowing against him, her face pressing against his chest. "So much blood."

"It's the way of war, Emily, and don't let anyone tell you different—this is war."

"They had such grand plans," she

mourned. Yet sleep was already tugging at her again.

He slid his hand beneath her shirt to caress her gently rounded backside. "Emily."

"Mmmmm?" The sound was both question and soft purr of delight.

"I know just the thing to take your mind off it."

"I begin to think that is your cure for all ills."

"It sure does wonders for what ails me," he growled softly.

"We should sleep," she tried to protest even as she arched to his touch as he cupped her breast in his hand.

"It'll help you sleep as well." His pulses leapt when she giggled softly.

To his delight, she held nothing back, participating and responding with equal abandon. He had an idea that it was a momentary surrender and took full advantage of it. There was little doubt in his mind that her subtle but ever-present resistance would return later.

Emily was a little shocked by her actions but quickly dismissed the fear that she was some kind of wanton. She knew she was using the physical magic he had introduced her to in order to erase her memories, if only temporarily. It also helped her fall asleep, a deep peaceful sleep that, for now, was not haunted by memories of a blood-soaked campsite.

"Poor little Emily," Cloud murmured as

he studied her asleep in his arms, looking like a child in his large shirt.

It never ceased to amaze him how so many people, raised in the east and accustomed to its settled civilization, could pick up and march west. So few of them had any idea of what they would face or how to take care of themselves. With wives and children in tow, men set out with their heads full of dreams and little common sense. Unfortunately, it was people like Emily and Thornton who suffered as a result of their folly.

For all he had seen of death and battle, despite how it had hardened him, the suffering of the innocents never ceased to affect him. They were always caught up in the maelstrom, suffering and not understanding why. Too often they died or were permanently scarred in mind or body or both. Emily's sleep was too often haunted and the boy, who even now crept toward them, was also disturbed by a memory he was too young to fully understand.

"Can I share, Mr. Ryder?"

Cloud looked at the little boy who knelt by the bed clutching his blanket. Thornton was wide-eyed and close to crying. Emily's presence during the night had no doubt been keeping the worst of his fears away. Cloud shifted himself and Emily to make room for the child.

"Sure. Climb in, boy. You can't make a habit of this, though."

"I know." Thornton scrambled in and

sidled up close to the sleeping Emily. "Mama said that."

"This Mama?" Cloud ventured.

"Yup. My first one's wif the angels. Are you gonna be my second papa?"

"No," Cloud replied gently. "Think of me as an uncle if you want."

"Okay. I never had one of them." He snuggled a little closer to Emily. "This is nice. Mama's warm."

"That she is, Thornton," Cloud drawled, smiling to himself.

"Are you going to keep the Injuns away?"

"I'll do my best. Let's say I'll try to keep us away from the Indians."

"That's good. I don't want Mama to hafta dig no more holes."

"Neither do I, son. Now get to sleep. We've still got a long way to go."

Thornton obediently closed his eyes but asked, "Is it pretty in Sandly's?"

"Yes, it's a real pretty place. You'll be happy there, Thornton. Now sleep."

As Thornton worked to obey that command, Cloud thought of the valley. After the war, he had done a lot of wandering and had chanced to find himself in the San Luis Valley. Even though he had not been ready to settle there, he had marked out his land, knowing that was where he would want to be when he grew tired of roaming. His younger brother Wolfe did settle and, for nearly three years, had kept a watch on both lots of land.

He now felt like doing something with the acres he had marked out. The winter would give him the time to sort out exactly which of his many ideas was the best. Over the years he had gathered a nest egg he felt was large enough to let him do as he pleased.

With thoughts of building a home to the fore of his mind, he suddenly found himself thinking of filling it. When his gaze fell upon Emily and Thornton he was a little disconcerted. The pair was having an unsettling effect upon him, threatening to soften too many of his hard edges.

His gaze still fixed upon the woman and child curled up next to him, he reviewed the idea that had flashed through his mind. In truth, he decided it was not at all that illogical. When a man put down stakes and built a house, it was usually with a family in mind. Despite his aversion to tying himself to a woman, he had always wanted children and had reluctantly accepted the fact that a wife was needed for that.

Emily was no frontierswoman, but she was strong and willing to learn. She had also been a virgin and, despite what he had told her, that did work in her favor. So too did that touch of puritan in her. Cloud felt confident that there would be no need to guess who'd fathered any child she gave him.

Since he was not a man given to romantic notions, he viewed the matter with a cool practicality. It began to look a very sensible course. With a last look at Emily, he closed

amazed her that she was not absolutely exhausted.

It was neither of those things that truly bothered her, however. What was beginning to frighten her was that the small resistance she did put up was getting harder to maintain. So was an attitude of aloofness. He was slowly possessing far more than her body, and it had not been quite a full week since she met him. Sometimes the shame she felt was so strong it cramped her stomach, but it never stopped her from melting into his arms at night. She trembled to think what the state of her emotions would be by the time they reached the San Luis Valley. Nothing she did seemed to halt her heedless fall into love.

When they dismounted near the supply depot's meager stable inside the blockade, she got further proof of how much danger she was in. A well-formed redhead burst out of the building, flung her arms around Cloud, and proceeded to give him a hearty kiss that he did little to stop. Emily felt anger and pain knot inside of her and knew she was blindingly jealous.

"Here now, Justine, let a man catch his breath." Cloud gently but firmly extracted himself from the woman's hold.

"Asphyxiation would suit you," muttered Emily as she began to undo her saddle.

Cloud pretended not to hear that but took Justine by the arm and nudged her a step closer to Emily. "There's someone here you ought to meet. Emily Brockinger, Justine Dubois."

"How do you do, Miss Dubois." Emily saw no reason to not at least be polite.

Justine glared at her. "How do and it's Missus."

"Is it?" Emily asked softly, not stopping in the removing of the saddle from Carolynn.

"Yeh, it is. I'm a widder." Justine smoothed the skirts of her bright blue dress.

"I should have guessed," Emily murmured. "Your grief is so apparent."

"Who the hell's she?" Justine snapped, turning a narrow-eyed gaze upon Cloud.

"My traveling companion," he drawled, putting an arm around Emily and bending toward her.

Emily held the saddle between them. "Don't you dare put those much-used lips anywhere near my mouth."

"Jealous, sweetheart?" he asked coolly.

"Not by a long shot, *darling*. I simply cherish my good health."

"Our bargain—"

"—said nothing about my having to stand docilely by and be made to look like a raving jackass," she hissed as she pulled free of his light hold.

He rubbed his chin thoughtfully as he watched her see to the care of her saddle. When he noticed how her little chin was up, he grinned. She did have a point. It certainly did make one feel a fool when the one you had ridden in with was busy carrying on with another. As he mulled over the matter, Cloud remained oblivious to the man at his side, who had heard the exchange and was struggling to overcome his surprise.

"Any time you can tear yourself away from deciding which miss to bless with your attentions, a hello would not be amiss."

"James!" Cloud cried, turning to his old friend. "What the hell are you doing here?" He frowned as he surveyed James's outfit while shaking his hand. "Where's your uniform?"

"Ah, well, that fool wanted me to lead the men. Gave me a choice—go or resign." James shrugged his broad shoulders. "I resigned. Came here on the stage."

"So that's how you got here before us."

"Us?" James asked, his silver gaze revealing his puzzlement. "I thought you rode alone. Who's us?"

"Miss Emily Brockinger and"—he placed a hand on Thornton's head—"Thornton Sears. This is an old friend of mine, James Carlin."

Nodding to the man as she started to curry her horse, Emily murmured, "You are slipping, Mr. Ryder. That is a man."

"Don't be pert," he admonished with a grin.

"I wouldn't dream of it."

"How did you two happen to meet?" James asked.

"Well," Cloud drawled, "I crested this hill and saw this little lady stumbling along, parasol in hand, dragging the stubbornest mule I've ever set eyes on and carrying the boy on her back. Naturally, seeing such damned foolishness, out of the goodness of my heart, I went and set her right."

"I do believe I am going to be ill," Emily muttered and slapped the currying brush into his hand. "I am going to see what goods the storehouse provides."

"Need some money?"

She put her hands on her hips and glared up at him from beneath the brim of her bonnet. "I would not take your money if I was blind and maimed and propped up with a tin cup."

"Got some of your own then, hmmm? What're you buying?"

"New material for my parasol." She started towards the door of the storehouse.

"Think you're good enough to ride with the reins in one hand and the parasol in the other?"

"Not at all. I felt it would be useful for all those leisurely rest stops you give us."

"See what happens when you're kind, James? Nothing but base ingratitude."

"The day you are kind, Mr. Ryder, I shall keel over, lilies clutched to my bodice." She had just stepped inside the store when she called out, "Thornton? Coming?"

Cloud grinned at a laughing James as Thornton hurried after Emily. "Cute as hell, ain't she? Little witch."

"The girl thinks too much of herself," huffed Justine, tired of being ignored.

"There does not seem to be anyone here to accept my money. Does that mean that everything is free?" Emily called from within the store.

The two men laughed as Justine rushed into the store just as Emily had clearly known she would. James then turned his hand to aiding Cloud in the care of the animals and cart. Cloud kept him well entertained with the full tale of how Emily had looked when he first saw her.

"Just can't see you dragging a city-bred girl and a little boy along with you."

"It has its compensations," Cloud said as they entered the store to find Emily bent over a box of ribbons and he patted her backside.

"Do that again and I shall do you a serious injury."

"Got a sharp tongue, doesn't she," James observed as they took a seat at a table in the half of the building that served as a tavern. "She certainly doesn't cling like your others."

"Nope, Emily's no clinger. Three beers and something for the boy, Justine." He smiled crookedly when Justine left the table with invitation in her every sway. "She's in a tiff just now."

"Leaving another behind, are you?"

"Oh, no. I'm taking her and the boy to the valley. That's where she was headed when I found her. No, Em's just miffed because I kissed Justine when I arrived—or rather, Justine kissed me and I allowed it." He took a sip of the beer Justine set down before him. "Very good, Justine. Could you ask Emily and Thornton to come over here?"

"Is she a friend of yours or something?"

Cloud thought over the last few days of traveling with Emily. He was a little surprised to find that he could not think of one moment when he had been bored or had wished to be rid of her. Despite the fact that she was still learning many of the simple basics needed to stay alive in a still untamed territory, she was a very good companion.

"Yeh, Justine, she's a friend of mine."

"A friend, huh?" marveled James after Justine had flounced away. "Maybe that's not such a good thing if she's the jealous sort."

"Don't know if it was jealousy, but she was definitely angry. Said it made her look a fool and she's got a good dose of stiff-necked Yankee pride. Thinking it over, she's right and Emily doesn't deserve to be made a fool of. She doesn't know a damn thing about surviving out here and admits it, but she was doggedly pushing on anyway when I spotted her. Many another lady would've sat down and wept. For all her tart remarks, she doesn't bitch either."

"A high accolade indeed," murmured James as Emily and Thornton arrived.

Emily sat down between the two men and Thornton scrambled up onto the chair opposite her. She was trying very hard not to be angry, but Justine's behavior was not helping. The woman did not know about the deal between her and Cloud, yet she was acting as if she would be taking Emily's place while they were at the fort. For all her remarks about being unwilling, Emily knew that that arrangement would sorely hurt and infuriate her. If nothing else, it would make her look the expedient bedwarmer she was trying hard to deny she was.

"What's this?" she asked, studying the drink before her.

"Beer. Don't tell me you've never had beer?"

"All right, Cloud. I won't." She took a sip. "It's rather nice."

"Just what'd you drink back in Boston?"

"Tea, lemonade, an occasional glass of sherry. Beer or ale was a drink for a working gentleman."

Cloud rolled his eyes in disgust. "Didn't your sister's husband work?"

"As little as possible," Emily replied, her eyes alight with deviltry. "Work is so *common*, you know."

"Never did understand the rich. Whole

different species. Justine," Cloud called, "still serve meals?"

"Yup." She sidled over to press against his shoulder. "I have a fine stew on the menu today."

He shifted so that the contact was broken. "Sounds fine. Can we have four bowls, please?"

Over the meal, which even Emily had to admit was good, James kept her talking about Boston. He had never been that far east and was honestly interested in a life that seemed to be lived in another world. He thought, too, that Emily's world in Boston had been that of the financially well-off.

Thanks to James's pleasant talk, and another tankard of beer, Emily's mood improved. The arrival of a few more travelers kept Justine busy, which suited Emily just fine. It was a while before she realized that the beer was far more potent than she had thought.

"Where are we to sleep tonight?" she asked Cloud.

Grinning, for he suspected she was beginning to feel the effects of too much beer, Cloud drawled, "Why, Em, sweet, are you that eager?"

She scowled at him. "Your crudity is excelled only by your vanity."

James snickered softly and Cloud grinned wider, then called, "Justine?"

That woman abruptly left the two young

soldiers she had been flirting with. "Yeh, Cloud?"

"You still have those two private rooms upstairs for hire?"

While Cloud and Justine haggled over the price, Emily's gaze went to the two young soldiers. One of them was eyeing her, but the other was glaring at Cloud's back. Emily felt sure that the young man was more than casually acquainted with Justine and resented her fawning attentions to Cloud. She also felt sure that he was within a breath of starting a fight. When she saw how Justine kept glancing toward the soldiers as she pressed against Cloud, Emily knew the woman was goading the poor young man.

She was just about to say something concerning Justine's game when the soldier broke free of his companion's restraining hold and lunged. "Look out, Cloud! Behind you."

Cloud had already stood and turned to meet the attack when she cried out. She, James, and Thornton barely escaped going down with the table as the two grappling men crashed down on top of it. Emily noted sourly that Justine had anticipated the soldier's move and stepped well out of the way. She now stood avidly watching the fight.

"Are you all right, miss?" James asked.

"Just fine. They ought to be thrashing her instead of each other."

"Started it, did she?" James looked at

Justine. "She's sure enjoying herself."

"Is there no way to stop this?"

"Not that I know of," he said, then added, "It's taking longer than it should though. I think Cloud's trying not to hurt the young fool."

Looking at the soldier's battered face, Emily drawled, "Really? How kind."

For a short while she stood by doing nothing, wincing at each blow that landed and scowling at the small, avidly watching crowd. She finally decided that she had had more than enough of two grown men pummeling each other for the gratification of a vain woman. Slipping away from James, she took a hasty tour of the place and was rewarded in her search.

Walking back to where Cloud and the soldier wrestled on the floor, she got as close as she dared and tossed the contents of the bucket on them. The cold water did the trick. They separated and sat up spluttering, allowing James and the other soldier to dash in and physically stop them from starting up again. Emily noted that, with some of the blood washed away, they were not as battered as she had first thought.

"What the hell did you do that for?" growled Cloud as he wiped his face with the towel James had fetched.

"It was becoming tedious, Mr. Ryder. Now, if you had been fighting for a worthy cause—"

"He was after Justine!" expounded the

soldier. "I was fighting for her."

Emily looked at the preening woman with a contempt that made Justine flush with anger. "This? To the victor goes the spoils?"

"Here now!" shrilled Justine.

"Mrs. Dubois," Emily interrupted icily, "if you must satisfy your vanity by having men beat each other to a pulp over your disputable charms, that is your privilege. However, Mr. Ryder is my guide and guard. He would be of little use to me if he was beaten senseless."

"Phew," James breathed. "That sure cut Justine down a notch or two."

Cloud grinned. "Em can talk like a damn duchess. She better watch it, though. Justine's got a fierce temper."

"It ain't his guiding and guarding you're fretting about," Justine hissed, "but that he'll get too beat up to serve you in bed."

Emily stared coldly at Justine. In truth, she had not been all that concerned for Cloud. The younger, more slightly built soldier had been little threat to him. Her disgust had been all for Justine, and she had simply wanted to stop the fight that had fed her vanity.

"Justine," Cloud said in a soft warning as he stood up.

"What's she got to be so high and mighty for? She's nothing but your whore."

That stung and Emily said, in a soft clipped voice, "Your remarks reveal your low breeding."

The slap Justine delivered nearly sent Emily to the floor. Emily reacted to the attack without any real thought, bringing forth lessons learned when, as a child ignored by her family, she had sought playmates among the children of the servants, children who had put her through many a trial before accepting her and had left her with an almost permanent black eye. As she had done so often back then, she balled up one small fist and delivered a sound right to Justine's jaw. The taller woman fell unconscious with a soft grunt.

"Well, I'll be damned," Cloud said quietly, staring at the sprawled Justine.

"Undoubtedly." Realizing with she had done, Emily began to feel sorely embarrassed.

"Didn't learn that at a tea party," he observed with a grin.

"No. From the stableboy."

"What the hell's going on here?" bellowed a deep voice.

James hustled Emily and Thornton back to the table he had set right. Cloud took over the chore of talking to the huge bearded man who was Justine's father. Justine's brother took her to her room and then took over the job of serving beer. Emily did not really think she wanted another glass but began to drink it anyway, for it soothed the intense embarrassment she felt. It was several moments before Cloud returned to the table, still grinning from his exchange with

Justine's father.

"We've got two rooms. You're welcome to share with Thornton, James."

Emily felt color flood her face and tried to hide it by taking a drink. She did not doubt that James had already assumed that she shared Cloud's bed. It was, however, a little disconcerting to hear it referred to so casually.

"Think I'll take you up on that. In fact, I was hoping to join you on your journey."

"Planning on settling in the valley?"

"Maybe. Whether I find something there or not, I'd like to see the place I've heard you lauding for years."

"I'd welcome your company—and your gun. We're starting out early in the morning. Got to keep pushing or we'll have to race the coming of the snows."

"Fine with me." He looked at Thornton. "Mind if I share your bed?"

"Nope. I like company and he stoled Mama."

When Emily groaned softly, both men stifled a laugh. She hurriedly excused herself and Thornton, saying the boy needed to put to to bed. Following Cloud's instructions, she found her way to the two rooms where their bags had already been stowed.

"Are you gonna sleep with dat udder man, too?" asked Thornton.

"Certainly not," gasped Emily as she hastily tucked the boy into his bed.

"It'll be real good having anudder man."

"Yes. Yes, it will. Mr. Ryder is quite capable, but it never hurts to have added protection."

She sat down on the bed and told him the bedtime story that had become a ritual, but tonight grew a little silly as a result of the beer she'd drunk. Emily was afraid that all the giggling they indulged in would keep him awake, but Thornton was asleep before she had finished folding his clothes.

Looking down at the sleeping boy, she briefly contemplated staying with him. Then she sighed and started toward the room allotted to her and Cloud. He would simply pick her up and tote her to his bed. It was a form of resistance that was not worth the effort. The man did not seem to understand what he was doing to her sense of morals, nor did he seem to be interested in her quandary.

Undressing proved more difficult than usual. She alternated between giggling over and cursing at her sudden incompetence. The last of her clothing had just dropped to the floor when she heard footsteps; she leapt into bed, pulling the covers up to her neck just as Cloud entered the room.

"Just what I like—the woman all ready and waiting," he drawled as he latched the door.

"Do you never knock when you enter a bedroom?" she grumbled.

"Not too often. Especially not when it's my bedroom," he said cheerfully as he began to undress.

Try as she would, she could not take her gaze from his body as he undressed and washed. He really was a glorious example of manhood. Her gaze moved with ill-hidden appreciation from his broad shoulders over his slim hips and on down his long, muscled legs. She suddenly sensed his gaze on her and hers flew up to meet his, finding his brown eyes decidedly warm.

"Like what you see?" He slipped into bed and reached for her.

"Yes," she blurted out and blushed furiously, knowing she had had too much to drink.

He immediately guessed that she was somewhat tipsy and grinned even while he felt unusually flattered. The drink had released her inhibitions even though there was still enough of the old Emily there to be startled by her own words. He knew she meant what she said even if she had not really wanted to say it. The idea of Emily liking how he looked pleased him far more than he thought it ought to. When she started to move her hand over his chest, he stopped thinking about it. Plainly, more than her control of her tongue had been affected. Cloud turned his thoughts to finding out just how little reserve she had left.

"You really are an extraordinarily hand-some man," she murmured, then groaned when she realized what she had said.

Cloud smiled into her hair. "What about my scar?"

"It makes you look like a real devil. How did you get it? A woman, I should imagine."

"Well, there was a woman involved." His voice grew increasingly hoarse as she moved her hands over his body slowly and shyly, almost exploringly. "She was married, but even at nineteen I wasn't one to turn my back on something freely offered. Her husband caught us."

"That poor man," she whispered as she slid her hands over his smooth slim hips. "You fought?"

"Yes," he croaked as her touch reached his thighs. "Right there in his bedroom."

Emily was fascinated by the changes, however subtle, that his growing passion made on his face. His strange eyes burned into hers, the amber ring seeming to grow brighter. She knew the drink was prompting her feeling of sensual abandon, but she could not seem to gain control of herself.

"You did not kill him, did you?" she breathed as she brought her stroking hands to the juncture of his thighs.

"No," he ground out. "He cut me and the woman's screams brought the servants. In the confusion, I grabbed my clothes and ran. God, that feels good, honey. Such a sweet touch."

"I'm feeling very wanton," she said with an odd mix of shame and delight. "Is it the drink?''

"If it is, I'm taking a keg along with us," he growled against her throat.

A tap at the door interrupted his progress toward her breasts. Emily flopped onto her back with a disappointed sigh. Cloud sat up, but his gaze remained fixed on her. He was fascinated with an Emily whose sensuality was in full control of her lithe body.

"Who is it?" he called crossly, shivering when Emily ran her hand over his lower back.

"Justine," hissed a voice in reply. "Why have you locked the door? You've never done that before."

"I wanted privacy," he gasped, burying his hand in Emily's hair when she began to trail kisses over his hip and thigh and urging her towards a spot that ached for her kisses.

"She's in there, isn't she?" Justine snapped, striking her fist against the thin door.

"God," he groaned when Emily obeyed his urgings. "She certainly is. Go away, damn it."

"You're a real bastard, Cloud Ryder," Justine shrilled before stomping off down the hall.

Cloud fell back onto the bed and Emily looked down at him. "That wasn't very nice."

"I've never been known for my diplomacy. Damn, but you're beautiful. Come here," he growled as he yanked her into his arms. "I knew this was what you could be, honey. You don't need the drink to bring it out." He rolled so that she was beneath him. "If only you'd stop being such a little puritan."

"It's my heritage," she breathed, arching to the touch of his eager hands. "Oh, Cloud, please. Please."

He did not need to be asked so eloquently; he was more than ready to take possession of her. Stirred beyond anything he could recall, his lovemaking was fierce, but Emily met it with a ferocity of her own. Their cries of release blended in the dimly lit room. They held onto each other tightly while they drifted back to earth and their sated bodies stopped trembling.

Although he eased the intimacy of their embrace, Cloud stayed sprawled on top of her, his head pillowed on her breasts. "Ah, little Emily, if only you'd let go more often. It's so damn good."

"Yes, it is, isn't it," she murmured, too close to sleep to care about the voice in her head that groaned in disgust over her unthinking admission.

"Is that yours?" the woman nearly screeched, pointing at Thornton.

It took but one instant's thought for Emily to decide that she did not like the woman. To refer to sweet little Thornton as a 'that' was more than she could tolerate. Only her distaste for putting herself in the middle of Cloud and another one of his women halted her.

"This is Thornton, Pamela," Cloud said coolly. "What are you doing here?"

"My father was given a new post." Pamela continued to eye Thornton with distaste. "I was afraid you would never get the word about where I was, but here you are."

"Pure miserable mischance."

"He can be a little unkind," Emily murmured to James.

"Very unkind. Shall we see to the horses?"

Nodding, Emily helped James tend to the horses and mule. They were done and wondering what to do next before Cloud was able to extract himself from an increasingly angry Pamela. It was clear from the expression on his face that she had left him in a sour mood. Emily hoped it would not last long.

To her relief Cloud's mood improved quickly as he talked to a disreputable-looking man called Jack. Although she politely thanked the man for his generosity when he lent them his cabin, Emily wondered if it was going to look as seedy as he did. She found herself pleasantly surprised when they entered the small two-room cabin, for it was shining clean and homey, something she credited Jack's Indian wife with.

"Are you certain we are not inconveniencing that man and his wife too much?" Emily set her bag on the huge bed.

"Very certain. They were just headed out to visit her kin."

"Visit the Indians? They won't kill him, will they? I mean, they must know that he scouts for the Army."

"No, they won't kill him." He kissed her cheek and started out of the room. "Her tribe is peaceful. Has to be. Near to two-thirds of them died of smallpox two years back. I'm just going to see the major. Won't be long. Come on, James."

"Knock before you come back in," she called after them. "I intend to make use of that tub I saw."

Looking back into the room, Cloud drawled, "You may need some help scrubbing your back."

"Somehow I doubt that. The major awaits you."

"I'll take Thornton."

"Thank you."

When she finally slipped into the tub of hot water, she nearly groaned with pleasure. It seemed years since she had been able to enjoy a hot bath. She soaked idly for just a little while, then began to get on with the business of bathing, for she did not fully trust Cloud to respect her privacy or cater to her modesty.

Just as she stepped out of the tub and started to dry herself off there came a single sharp rap at the door. She gave a squeak of surprise and, clutching her towel, raced for the bedroom when the door opened. Cloud relentlessly strode after her. When she turned to scold him for his total lack of consideration for her sense of modesty, the words never left her lips. She thought the look on his face a very disturbing one. There was an intensity about him that sent a shiver through her.

"Emily." She looked so clean, so alive, he ached for her.

"Is something wrong, Cloud?" His voice was hoarse and thick, yet she sensed it was not wholly passion that made it so.

"Wrong?" He laughed and did not need her wide-eyed look to know the sound was unpleasant. "Yeh, you could say that."

"Cloud?"

"Sssh, Em. Please. No words. Not now. Not yet."

Before she could again ask him what was wrong, however, he grabbed her, tossed her onto the bed and began making fierce, silent love to her. When Emily's mind was finally cleared of passion's grip and she still held his heavily breathing body close, she found herself torn between confusion and hurt. As always, the pleasure had been sweet and all-consuming and the guilt she could never fully shake tickled at her. This time, however, she felt badly used. Not only had he said nothing, but she had the strong feeling that every caress had been calculated to stir her quickly so that he could have his pleasure quickly. Never before had he left her feeling so much a part of a bargain— as she was—and nothing more.

Cloud sighed but did not lift his head from where it rested against her breasts. He did not particularly want to see the look on her face. The tension in her body told him he would not like it.

"Sorry, Em. I used you poorly and you don't deserve that."

"Why?" she asked softly, hoping there was a reason good enough to dispel her hurt.

"I'm not sure. I heard some news at the major's and just knew I had to get back here. Then, when I saw your cute pink backside disappearing into this room, I knew what I needed, knew what was the sweetest, surest cure for the feelings gripping me so fierce."

"What did the major tell you?"

"Have you heard me and James talking on why we left the fort?"

"Yes, that officer wanted to do something you had both warned him was foolish— something that was certain to get him and his men killed." She held him a little tighter, suddenly understanding what troubled him so. "He did it, didn't he?"

"He did." Cloud spoke through clenched teeth as he fought his returning fury. "He rode out with his whole troop. Three got back, Em. Only three and one of them, worst luck, was him. I wanted to ride right back there and kill him—kill him like he killed all those poor fools he ordered to their deaths. Maybe if James and I had stayed . . ."

"It would have mattered not a jot. You were not his commanding officer. You could only advise, not order. The fact that he would not listen to someone with experience and knowledge shows that he meant to do exactly what he wished to, no matter what was said. You can be sure that every man with him wished he could have left as well, if he could have done so without being accused of desertion. They had no choice. You did, and they would have thought you a fool for acting otherwise."

Lifting his head, he briefly kissed her, then smiled faintly. "That was what I was after—comfort. Good sense told me there was nothing I could have done besides getting killed myself, but you don't think clear when you hear such news for the first time." He sighed. "I just wish there was something I could do now to be sure that incompetent idiot doesn't get any more chances to waste lives."

"Isn't there? I do not know all that much about the military but, when an officer errs, or appears to have erred, is there not an inquiry?" She had to smile at the arrested look that came over his face, for she had rarely surprised him like that; but then he surprised her by giving her a brief, hard kiss and leaping out of bed.

"I have to go talk to the major again," he muttered as he yanked on his clothes.

Realizing what had caused him to act so abruptly, she relaxed. "Where are James and Thornton?"

"They went to get supplies. Best drag out your finest, sweetheart. We dine with the major tonight and there's a small party."

She had no time to ask for any details, for he hurried from the room, still buttoning his shirt. Sighing, she got to her feet and started to get dressed. She did not really want to accept the invitation, for it would undoubtedly mean another awkward confrontation with Pamela. Telling herself not to be a coward, she began to plan what she would wear, something that proved quite difficult despite her paucity of choices. She had to smile at herself when she realized that she was really struggling over the best way to outshine the beauteous Pamela.

Cloud sipped his whiskey and scowled at the dancers—at one couple in particular. The major was paying far too much attention to Emily. Worse, in Cloud's mind, Emily seemed to be thoroughly enjoying it. Up until the man had first taken Emily off to dance, Cloud had liked Major John Leeds. Now he felt a keen urge to drag the man outside and beat him soundly.

When he felt someone touch his arm, he dragged his attention away from Emily and scowled at Pamela. She had become a real

HANNAH HOWELL

nuisance, spending all evening pinching at
Emily and flirting outrageously with him.
The woman was oblivious, or seemed to be,
to his clear lack of interest. He thought
crossly that, if Emily stayed close at hand,
Pamela would cease to be a problem, for he
could make his refusal to play her games
visual as well as verbal. Never before had he
felt a need to use one woman as a shield
against another, but the idea strongly
appealed to him at the moment, for Pamela
was pressing him hard, backing him into a
corner.

Glancing toward Emily, who laughed gaily
at something the major said, Cloud wondered why he was being so reticent. Before,
whenever a woman had made it clear that
she was willing, he had been willing as well.
They offered; he took. It had been as simple
as that. Emily was simply another in a long
line of women, none of whom he had ever
been remotely faithful to.

The problem, he thought angrily, was
that he did not want to reach out and take
what Pamela was hurling at him. He took a
deeper drink of his whiskey and admitted
that he wanted only Emily. It did nothing to
improve his temper and his replies to
Pamela's attempts at conversation grew curt,
almost vicious.

Major John Leeds smiled down at the slim
woman in his arms. "I must say, Miss Emily,
I was surprised to find a woman like you
with Cloud. Pleasantly surprised, of course."

"How kind. Mr. Ryder not only saved my life and Thornton's, for I am certain we never would have lasted on our own, but he is escorting us to my brother. I believe he explained it?"

"Oh, Cloud helping out like that is no surprise."

"It isn't?"

"No. He's well known for rescuing people in trouble. Put his own life in jeopardy more times than I can count. Even followed some Comancheros for hundreds of miles once to bring back some young girls they had stolen. You were lucky to have stumbled upon him, Miss Emily."

"Yes, it would seem so," Emily managed to reply in a strangled voice.

Several different emotions warred with each other inside her. She was glad the man she was so involved with was not as cold and callous as he pretended. But she was furious that he had played such a game with her. And she was hurt that he would use her so. Rage overwhelmed her for a moment and she thought of immediately confronting Cloud. Yet, to her confusion, she hesitated.

"I'm just sorry it wasn't me who found you."

The major's voice pulled her free of her confused thoughts. The middle of a crowded dance floor was no place to make a decision on what she had learned. Firmly, she set the knowledge aside to be mulled over later. Neatly avoiding the major's attempts to draw her closer as they danced, she concentrated on enjoying the celebration.

Major Leeds really was a rogue, she thought with an inner smile. It had annoyed her at first, even frightened her a little, but her mood had swiftly improved. Part of that had come about as she realized that he was not after some woman he thought free with her favors, something Emily had feared he thought because of her place with Cloud. The man was simply an incorrigible flirt who thought he had new, fertile ground to explore yet did not get angry when she turned aside his ploys.

What truly lifted her spirits was that she was discovering something very important about herself. Nothing the major did produced any more than the pleasant feeling one could get from flattery and the attentions of a handsome man. Not the slightest hint of desire or wantonness flickered through her veins. The sense of relief she felt left her almost light-headed.

One thing that had continuously troubled her, if in varying degrees of intensity, was how swiftly she had succumbed to passion with Cloud. When he held her, she lost all reticence and her morals became non-existent, only returning later to haunt and scold her for her weakness. She had begun to fear that she suffered from a weakness of the flesh, that she could be one of those women who were little better than whores. Her reactions, or, rather, the lack of them, to the major proved that a groundless fear. Her weakness was simply Cloud Ryder. He was the only one who could so easily undermine all her principles.

Still giggling over an outrageous piece of flattery from the major, Emily let him escort her to the punch bowl. She was just accepting a drink from him when Cloud appeared at their side, a grinning James with him. Her smile of welcome faltered slightly when she noticed how stern Cloud was looking; then it faded completely when Pamela appeared at Cloud's side, slipping her arm possessively through his.

Sternly, Emily told herself not to give in to the jealousy surging through her. Pamela, however, was proving to be a far greater trial than any of the other women. For one thing, Cloud did not seem to be brushing the woman aside. Emily felt a flicker of fear but fought to subdue it. So far Cloud had not turned to any of the other women that had been so obviously willing. She would trust him to continue to stay by her unless he blatantly moved to do otherwise.

"Emily," James said cheerfully as he stepped closer to her, "I haven't had the pleasure of dancing with you yet."

"And a great pleasure it is, too," the major said quietly and kissed Emily's hand.

"You are too kind, Major. Well—" Emily quickly finished off her drink, set her glass down and hooked her arm through James's— "shall we see to correcting that lapse?"

"Best we had."

"Emily."

She looked at Cloud, who was still looking stern. This puzzled her. "Something wrong?"

"That punch was doctored. It might be wise if you go easy on it." He could tell by the brightness of her eyes and the slight flush on her cheeks that she had already had more than enough.

"Doctored? Oh. You mean someone had added spirits to it. That explains why it tastes so sparkling. Come along, James." She towed a chuckling James out onto the dance area.

"A delightful young woman, Cloud."

"I noticed you thought so, John."

"A true lady."

Cloud frowned as he heard censure in the major's tone. "Spit it out, John. We've never minced words before." He noticed the major glance towards Pamela, whose presence he had forgotten, and he scowled at her, roughly freeing his arm from her grasp. "Don't you have some place to go?" He almost sighed with relief when, clearly deciding she had had enough, she flounced away. "You were saying, John?"

John sighed and shook his head. "When there's so many willing, easy ones about, why are you after Emily?"

"I'm not after Emily. I have her."

"Cloud, we aren't speaking about a woman like Pamela here."

"You think I don't know that?"

"You seem determined to work yourself

up into a temper. You won't goad me into stepping outside. I have no intention of coming to fisticuffs with you over this, but I mean to have my say. I don't like the game you're playing this time. She's a sweet, well brought-up girl and you could ruin her. She doesn't deserve that."

"No, she doesn't."

The major frowned. "Now I think you are playing games with me."

"Not at all. What's between Em and me is just that—between Em and me."

"I find it difficult to step back and let you turn that girl into a whore."

"John, nothing I could ever do to Em would make her become one of those. Leave it be, John. And leave her be, too," he added coldly. "Em's mine." He realized that he meant that wholeheartedly and wondered if he looked as surprised as John did. "I've got no intention of ruining her."

"No? You're making her name a scandal at every post and stop between where you started and the valley. That could easily catch up with her."

"Then I'll be there to divert it."

"You mean to stay with her?"

"I believe I do." He frowned when James returned to their side without Emily. "Where's Em?"

"Stepped outside for a moment. She said she was feeling warm. I think the punch has gone to her head." James saw Pamela go out the same way Emily had and scowled. "Now, what's she up to?"

"Nothing good," Cloud grumbled and set off hoping to stop a confrontation that could cause him a great deal of trouble.

Emily sighed with pleasure as she sat down on a rough bench and a cool breeze eased the heat in her face. She was feeling both warm and lightheaded. It occurred to her that the 'doctored' punch she had had so much of could be the cause of that. She hoped some fresh air would instill her with a more sober attitude. The last thing she wished to do was to become drunk and foolish, an embarrassment to both Cloud and herself. Liquor, she reflected, was a troublesome thing.

And here comes another troublesome thing, she thought crossly as she spotted Pamela approaching her. Even the thought that Pamela was at least not still clinging to Cloud did not ease the annoyance Emily felt. The expression on Pamela's face told Emily that the woman wanted some sort of confrontation, most likely an unpleasant one. Emily decided that she was more than a little tired of facing Cloud's seemingly endless collection of discarded lovers. This time, she decided, she was not even going to try to be polite.

"I believe you can guess what I wish to speak to you about." Pamela crossed her arms over her chest and looked down at Emily.

"You look just like my old schoolteacher."

"What?"

"When you stare down your nose like that, you look just like Miss Teasdale."

"Stop talking nonsense. I've come to talk about Cloud."

"Ah, what a surprise. Know him well, do you?"

"Of course I do and I must say, it surprises me that he would take up with such a prim miss from the east. You can't possibly give him what he needs." She smiled with sweet remembrance. "He's all man."

"Every inch of him." A double entendre, Emily thought with surprise. I have just uttered my first double entendre. She wondered if she was learning a little too much from Cloud. "I believe you're trying to tell me that you've known Mr. Ryder very well indeed."

"Very well indeed. I have been his lover for years. No woman could know him as well as I do."

"Oh, I think I may have collected an idea or two. I think you'd best turn your interests elsewhere. Cloud seems very slow to come to the sticking point and you aren't getting any younger."

Pamela glared at her. "No woman in her right mind would give up a man like Cloud Ryder. So strong, so well-formed."

"Oh, quite. I particularly like his right leg."

"What?"

Cloud stopped just short of the two women, feeling as surprised as Pamela sounded. Then he started to smile. Emily was feeling the effects of the punch. Recalling how she was after a few drinks of beer he wondered, with an inner laugh, if it might be a kindness to warn Pamela.

"His right leg." A small part of Emily reeled in shock and cried out in dismay over the way she was talking, but she was enjoying herself too much to heed it. "It is quite perfect, you know. I do not believe I have ever seen a man with a more perfect right leg."

Gritting her teeth, Pamela hissed, "You're trying to make a fool of me, but I won't stand for it. I suggest you find another way to travel and another man to take you."

"You mean, leave that beautiful right leg behind? Oh, I don't know if I could do that."

Since Pamela looked very close to striking Emily, Cloud decided he had best put a stop to the meeting. "Emily."

To her consternation, when Emily looked at Cloud she felt color heat her cheeks. It was one thing to be outrageous before a woman who annoyed her, quite another to have her slightly scandalous talk heard by a man, particularly the man she was talking scandously about. She heartily wished he would stop grinning so.

"Kind of you to keep Em company, Pamela, but we're headed back to the cabin now." Cloud took Emily by the hand and urged her to her feet. "Tell James when you get back inside." He watched Pamela flounce back inside and shook his head. "Sorry about that, Em."

"I believe I grow accustomed. My evening is over, is it?" The fresh air having done little to dispel the effects of the heady punch, Emily decided she would not complain.

"Quite," he murmured in teasing imitation of her way of speech. Then he picked her up in his arms.

"I can walk," she gasped as he strode off across the compound and she put her arms around his neck in a natural reaction to being off the ground.

"I know."

"Then why are you carrying me?"

"Let's call it a whim."

She blushed and hid her face in his neck when they entered the cabin to face the young girl Cloud had found to watch over Thornton. Emily was sure her name would be on everyone's lips by morning. Cloud seemed determined to make her a scandal. She sighed. By traveling with him as she was, she was no doubt already a scandal so there was no point in worrying over his occasional outrageousness.

Setting her down on her feet in the bedroom, Cloud moved to shut the door. "Now why are you frowning?"

"I'm frowning?"

"You were."

He sat down on the bed and tugged off his boots, watching her closely as she started to ready herself for bed. She looked every inch the fine lady in her rich blue gown, her hair done in what he assumed was the latest fashion back east. The major had had no difficulty in recognizing Emily for what she was—a young, well-bred lady caught up in circumstances beyond her control. Cloud supposed he ought to feel guilty about what he was doing to her and he did sometimes. Unfortunately, protecting her good name meant setting her aside, if only for the nights they spent at various outposts of civilization, and he was not about to do that.

What he could do, he decided, was try a little harder to keep the women he had known in the past away from her. There were several more places they had to stop at before they reached the valley. Unfortunately, there were also several more women. He was beginning to feel a little ashamed of his past. He was certainly beginning to heartily dislike the way Emily was constantly having to face that past. It would certainly not aid his cause if he asked her to marry him when they reached the valley, something he was more sure he would do with each passing day.

By the time he was undressed, Emily was standing in only her shift and taking down her hair. As he watched the thick, pale waves tumble free of their restraints, he felt his desire for her strengthen. Moving to stand behind her, he put his hands on her slim hips and nuzzled her thick, sweet-smelling hair.

"How is it you can be half-naked with your

hair down and still look so prim and lady-like?" he murmured as he picked her up in his arms and took her to the bed.

Staring at him as he lowered himself into her welcoming arms, she winced as she recalled Pamela's words. She *was* prim and there was a part of her that constantly wrung her hands in heartfelt shame whenever she made love with Cloud. There was little doubt in her mind that it affected their lovemaking, if only in a small way, because part of her was always holding back. That made her wonder if Pamela was right when the woman said she could not give Cloud all he needed.

She grew angry with herself when she heard herself ask softly, "But is prim what you need?"

Cloud knew who was to blame for that question and, as he tugged Emily's shift off, he decided it would serve him well to do what he could to ease any sting Pamela had inflicted. "Well, let's just see about that."

Sated and sleepy, her arms wrapped heavily around Cloud, who was sprawled on top of her, his head upon her breasts, Emily wondered how something so good could not be enough for any man. She also recalled something she had learned tonight, some-thing she had forgotten upon discovering that she was not really some indiscriminate wanton. Cloud had tricked her. It had really come as no surprise, but some tales the major had told her had clarified her suspicions. Cloud would never have left her and Thornton to struggle on alone.

Her first thought had been to confront him with the fact, to put an abrupt end to the shameful arrangement he had tricked her into. But it had only taken a moment's thought for her to admit that that was not really what she wanted to do. It would certainly never make her happy. She decided, as sleep started to gain a strong hold on her, that she would just leave things as they were.

"Emily?"

"Mmmm?"

"The answer's yes."

It took her a moment to figure out what he meant, then she smiled, feeling her heart skip a beat. If she had had any doubts about staying with him despite his trickery, he had just dispelled them.

real reason to stop them. He shrugged. "Go on, then. Just don't be too long and keep an eye out for any trouble."

"Yes, sir." Emily strongly suppressed the urge to salute as she turned and hurried away before he changed his mind.

"Come on, Cloud," James urged, laughing as he worked on the fire. "We haven't seen any sign of anything or anyone in days."

"I know. But I can't help but wonder if that's what troubles me." He sat before the fire. "Never liked it when it was so quiet."

"Well, Emily might not know too much about tramping across the wilderness, but she's not stupid. She'll keep an eye open and she won't stay away from us for too long. Brew the coffee," he ordered with a smile.

Although she ached to linger in the clean water, Emily regretfully rinsed herself off one last time and stepped out of the creek. Thornton handed her the towel, and she wrung out her hair and began to dry off. It was not until she had put on her clean underthings that she realized the child, once he had given her the towel, had wandered off. She sighed in slight exasperation when she saw that he had not gotten dressed yet.

Her exasperation quickly flared into fear when she could not immediately catch sight of him or get any reply to her soft calls. What she had first seen as naughtiness now took on the look of danger. She was just about to go for Cloud and James when she found the boy. Stepping through some thick brush, she saw Thornton's naked little body squirming in the firm hold of an Indian who was drawing very close to his pony. Once the Indian mounted, Emily knew in her heart that Thornton would be lost to her.

Frantically looking for something she could use as a weapon, she spied a thick piece of wood. Without a thought to her own personal safety or her lack of fighting skill, Emily raised her club and ran toward the Indian. She did not really aim or consider the best place to strike, but simply swung as soon as the Indian was in reach.

"Run, Thornton," she cried when the Indian cried out and dropped the boy. "Get Cloud and James. Go!"

As soon as the boy had run off, she turned her full attention to the Indian, who quickly recovered from his surprise. She decided that she did not like the way he looked at her, as if he were deciding that she would be a bigger prize than a little boy. Neither did she like not knowing what to do next. She thought it a little cruel for her mind to clear enough to remind her of her complete lack of fighting skills at such a moment.

The Indian brave looked very young but, to her dismay, he also looked fierce, strong and agile. Even if she had any real skill, she doubted it would do much good against him. Her only hope was that he faced her unarmed. It seemed that, whatever his plans were, he did not intend to murder her.

The Indian charged her. She swung her

club and struck him, but he barely faltered. With a soft cry, Emily was thrown to the ground. Her crude weapon was quickly lost as she was caught up in a frantic wrestling match. Despite her fierce struggle, she knew it would be a short battle and prayed that the men would come.

James saw Thornton first. "Good thing the sun's near set or that boy'd be burnt bad."

The smile that had begun to spread over Cloud's face when he first spotted the naked little boy faded quickly when Thornton cried, "Mama! Gotta go help Mama."

Catching hold of the boy, who nearly ran into him, Cloud demanded curtly, "What's happened to your mother?"

"An Injun grabbed me, then Mama hit him, and he's gonna grab her. Come on! You got to help!"

Cloud did not really need the boy's tugging on his arm to make him move. He stood up, caught Thornton up under his arm and started towards the creek at a steady lope, James at his heels. Thornton breathlessly directed them and answered Cloud's curt questions.

Once near the creek, Cloud set Thornton down and ordered the boy to stay put. He and James silently approached the spot where Thornton had last seen the brave, carefully watching in case there was more than the one Indian Thornton had seen. Despite their stealth and all Cloud's efforts

to restrain his first bloodthirsty impulse
when he saw the Indian handling Emily so
roughly, the Indian saw them before he and
James could act. With a snarl of fury, the
brave put Emily in front of him, one strong
arm wrapped tightly around her throat and
a knife pressed to her side.

Emily froze when she felt the pinch of the
knife at her side. It held her attention more
than the fact that the Indian's tight grip on
her throat threatened to cut off her air. Her
heart beat so fast it hurt. She looked at
Cloud, torn between wanting him to help and
wanting him to stay out of the matter for fear
he would put himself into grave danger.

"Easy, Cloud," James whispered. "Hell,
it's just a kid."

It took Cloud a moment to calm himself,
fear mixed with anger twisting his insides.
He was surprised at the emotions raging
through him when he saw the danger Emily
was in. In times of danger he had always
been known for his coolness, but it was
proving very difficult to stay cool this time.

As he brought himself under control, he
studied the Indian who held Emily. James
was right. He was a boy, although Cloud
knew the Indian was probably considered a
man by his people. It was very clear that the
Indian youth was man enough to appreciate
Emily. A little hard talking, perhaps some
bargaining, Cloud decided, was the safest
route to take.

When Cloud began to talk to the Indian in

a language Emily did not recognize in the least she was startled. The Indian gave a slight start as well, revealing that he shared her surprise and causing the knife to prick her skin. She hid her wince, afraid that any sign of distress or pain from her could only cause trouble. With every ounce of strength and willpower she had, Emily fought to at least look calm.

"He wants Em, doesn't he," James murmured when there was a pause in the negotiations.

"That's damn obvious," growled Cloud. "He ain't easy to talk to. Pigheaded youth."

"He holds the trump card."

"Not completely. He can't move, can't take his prize off and, if he hurts her, he's dead." A little crossly, Cloud told the Indian that in the youth's own tongue and felt a spark of hope when the youth frowned.

"You do not want the woman dead."

The mere thought of such a consequence sent a tremor of alarm through Cloud but none of that revealed itself in his voice when he spoke. "No, but I would rather her dead then taken by another. She is my woman." That tactic seem likely to work and he decided to stay with it.

It was several more moments of what was clearly a tense negotiation before Emily felt the Indian's hold on her start to ease. Whatever Cloud was telling the Indian it seemed to be working. She remained still, fighting the panicked urge to break free, for she knew the Indian would react quickly enough to get a firm hold on her again, perhaps even use the knife on her. When he suddenly let go of her, she was too startled to move; then she realized that he still had a firm grip on her hair.

"Cloud?"

"Easy, Em." He fixed a stern gaze upon the Indian. "I had to promise him some of your hair."

"My hair?"

"He thinks it'll be a powerful medicine."

Even as Cloud explained she felt one sharp tug on her hair. Clutching the place on her head where the pull had stung, she whirled around and caught one brief glimpse of the disappearing Indian, a hank of her pale hair clutched in his hand, before she was caught tightly in Cloud's arms. With one helpless look at him, she fainted.

"Em!" Cloud caught her up in his arms as she collapsed. "Emily?"

James hurriedly looked her over, then sighed. "Just a faint. Poor kid was scared clean to death, I'll bet. She just gave out." He hastened after Cloud as he strode back to camp.

"Mama! He killed my mama."

"She ain't dead, Thornton," Cloud said quietly as James picked up the frantic little boy. "She's just fainted."

"Fainted?" Thornton's gaze stayed fixed upon Emily even as he clung to James.

"Yes, it's like a little nap. She'll wake up

soon." He paused for a moment until James finished collecting their clothes, then started toward their camp again. "She just got too scared, Thornton. Woman's apt to do this when she gets real scared."

Although the boy looked calm he never took his gaze from Emily. Cloud gently set her down on the bedding he had laid out and Thornton squatted nearby. James quietly worked to get the boy dressed as Cloud did what little he could think of to rouse Emily.

Reaching up through the clouds of unconsciousness, Emily suddenly recalled the Indian and came awake with a start. Her fear eased when she saw only Cloud, James, and Thornton kneeling nearby and watching her. Then she recalled how the Indian had cut her hair and, with a soft gasp, she rose up on one elbow and smoothed her hand over the back of her head, trying to determine what damage had been done.

Realizing what was troubling her, Cloud also looked. "It's not bad, Em."

"I should be ashamed of such vanity," she grimaced, "but are you sure? It looked like he removed a great deal of hair."

"He did, but he slashed a top section. It should be easy to hide the missing part until it grows back. What the hell were you doing out here, anyway?"

Startled by his sudden cross demand and noticing how James and Thornton quickly deserted her, she stared at Cloud a little warily. "He was going off with Thornton."

"You could've called for help—for us."

"I did not think there was enough time for that, Cloud. I was afraid that, if he got away with Thornton, we would never get the boy back."

Sighing, Cloud nodded. "It wouldn't have been easy." He scowled. "It wasn't easy convincing him he didn't want you either."

She shivered faintly. Although everything had turned out all right, she knew all too well that it could easily have gone all wrong. There was no way she could have acted that would have changed things, however, so she offered no apology for her actions. In hopes of turning the subject, she started to sit up, only to realize that she was still dressed only in her underthings.

Blushing fiercely, she asked softly, "Where are my clothes?"

Biting back a smile, Cloud held out her dress. Despite all the time they had been together, all the lovemaking they had indulged in, Emily clung to her modesty. It was one of the things that never let him forget that this time he was dealing with a far different sort of female than he usually did. He liked it, even though there were times he wished she would set aside such notions, be a little freer. Then again, he mused, an unrestrained Emily could well set him back on his heels.

"You're not going to like this, Em," he said as he helped her do up her dress, "but that's the last time you and Thornton wander off alone. We were damned lucky this time. Next time . . ." He shrugged. "We're in a real wild area now and will be for a while."

She grimaced as he politely helped her stand. He was right. She did not like it. Nevertheless, she understood why he was imposing such a restriction. It was not only her or the boy at risk, but Cloud and James as well. She resigned herself to it as he led her to the fire where James had fixed their meal. There was a good chance that she would no longer feel safe going off by herself anyway.

"I think it'll be a good idea if we move on right after this," Cloud announced half-way through the meal.

"Think he might be back?"

"It's always a possibility, James."

Emily glanced at Thornton. He sat nearly in her lap quietly eating his food. She felt weighted down with the responsibility of the child, yet she knew in her heart that she would not give him up. What she did wish was that she could hurry up and get him to someplace that was safe and settled. Sighing, she looked back at the frowning men.

"You think there might be some trouble, don't you?"

"Best to act as if there will be, Em," Cloud said quietly. "It's wisest if we don't assume that he'll leave it at getting a hank of your hair, or that any of his tribe is too far away for him to get any help. Out here it's sometimes safer to always assume the worst."

"It will be dark soon. Won't that make travel dangerous?"

"A little. Damned slow too. It'll put us a good distance from here by daybreak, though, and give us a good head start if he comes after us with a few friends." He smiled faintly. "Don't look so worried, Em. We'll get you to Harper in one piece." Cloud knew, though, that he would be reluctant, very reluctant, to hand Emily over to Harper.

She smiled back, but it was little more than a polite response. She did want to get to someplace safe. She wanted the long, trouble-ridden journey over with. She also wanted to see her brother again. Unfortunately, to get all of those things meant the end of her time with Cloud and that was something she definitely did not want. But it was not something she was going to be given much choice about.

It was not long before they were repacked and traveling again. Emily watched Thornton nod off to sleep against Cloud and wished she could do the same. Novice though she was to riding, she knew it was going to prove to be a long, uncomfortable night.

The night was barely half over when Emily began to feel dangerously weary. She tried to fight sleep by thinking, concentrating her mind on everything and anything she could. It was not long before she wished she could indulge in the luxury of sleep, for the only thing her tired mind seemed inclined to concentrate on was Cloud and what seemed to be a doomed relationship. That was probably better than thinking about a horde of blood-crazed Indians swooping down upon them at any moment. She sighed again; thoughts of Indians brought fear, but thinking about Cloud brought the pain and sadness born of futility.

No matter how optimistic she tried to be, she could not talk herself into really believing that she was making much of an impression on Cloud's apparently well-protected heart. He gave no hint at all that their current relationship would become more stable. As they came closer to the San Luis Valley, his plan of leaving her with Harper never changed.

Her thoughts continued to circle round in her mind. She saw what could be hopeful signs in the way Cloud treated her, only to have that hope crushed by his lack of promises or even hints of other possibilities besides the inevitable separation. Her constant useless worrying of the problem brought her no solutions and soon it could not even keep her awake.

Several times she felt her chin touch her collarbone but jerked herself back into a semblance of wakefulness. She swallowed a plea to halt for a while. The men were plodding doggedly onward and she was determined to do the same even if it was growing painful to keep her eyes open.

The sky was just beginning to show hints of light when she lost her battle against sleep. Her mind was too clouded by exhaustion for her to use good, hard thinking as a means to stay awake. The steady plodding of her horse began to affect her as gently rocking cradle did a child. She had one brief flash of realization and cried out softly in frustration as sleep took a firm grip on her and she felt herself falling.

"Emily!" James hurriedly reined in his mount as he saw Emily fall.

Cloud looked back, even as he reined in. Cursing softly but viciously, he dismounted, pausing only to set the sleeping Thornton on the cart the mule pulled. He was crouching at Emily's side even as James put an arm beneath her shoulders and partly raised her from the ground. When her eyelids briefly lifted and she looked at him, he breathed a sigh of relief.

"Are you all right, Em?"

"Very sorry." She did not even try to fight it when her eyes shut again. "I simply could not stay awake another moment."

"Didn't you notice her getting exhausted?" Cloud crossly asked James.

"Nope. That little back was ramrod stiff right up until she fell. I think we'd better set here for a spell."

"We can't."

"Seen something?"

"Nope but, damn it, I smell it. I feel it. Don't know if it's that boy or if we're riding into something else. There's more'n enough mire around to step in."

"Charming. So why not just set here? Face whatever it is, if it comes?"

"I've got a better place up ahead."

"There's nothing up ahead but mountains."

"Exactly. We're going to go up into them for a while." He gently picked Emily up. "You can take the boy. Just give me a hand with Em."

He smiled faintly when she stirred slightly in his arms, cuddling up to him. Her subtle movement aroused him, yet it had not been very long at all since he had last made love to her. In fact, he mused, he had made love to Emily far more often than he had ever made love to any other woman before her, yet the hunger for her seemed as strong and swift as ever. Since he still thought it a good idea to marry her, that was good; yet it worried him a little for he could not help but see it as a power in her hands, a power easily misused if she ever fully realized that she held it.

As he mounted and then, with James's help, settled the soundly sleeping Emily before him, Cloud found himself thinking that Emily was not the kind of woman to misuse such a power. That surprised him, for he had hitherto had little trust in women. It was an attitude no woman had ever given him good reason to change. His first love had married the man her father chose for her, even as she declared undying love for him. Since then he had taken up with women like

Abigail, who used him as much as he used
them. A wife he could trust was not something he had ever held much hope of finding.

Glancing down at the young woman asleep
in his arms, Cloud decided it was time to find
out more about Harper. Emily had taken on
an arduous, dangerous trip to get to the man.
When she spoke of him, it was with affection,
although Cloud got the feeling that her
opinions and impressions of the man were
outdated ones. She had felt sure that Harper
would help pay him if he had charged her a
fee to guide her, and she felt sure that
Harper would be glad to see her, for he had
written to ask her to come. This Harper,
Cloud decided, could prove to be a sizable
obstacle. It was time to start finding out
exactly who the man was, exactly what he
meant to Emily, and what promises, if any,
had been exchanged.

"Cloud, are you sure you know where
we're going?" James said as he tightened his
grip on an increasingly restless, awakening
Thornton.

"Right up ahead."

"Looks like solid rock to me."

"There's a cave there."

"Livable?"

"If it hasn't crumbled."

"When did you last see it?"

"About a year ago. Last time I went to see
Wolfe." He gently shook Emily awake.
"Come on, Em, we have to lead the horses
from here."

It took Emily several minutes to wake up enough to see where they were. "What are we doing going up into the mountains?"

Helping her dismount, Cloud joined James in emptying the cart, dividing their belongings between the horses and the mule and hiding the cart. "To find a safe place to rest for a while. A cave. Secure, easy to defend, and dry."

"Might there not be some animal in there?"

"If there is, then we'll have some fresh meat for our supper." He glanced her way and laughed softly at the disgusted face she pulled. "Never had bear, huh?"

"A bear?" She put her arm around a yawning Thornton's shoulders and held the boy closer to her side. "Have you met one before?"

"Now, Em, a bear's not much to fret over."

"Easy enough for you to say," she grumbled as she took her mare by the reins and started to follow Cloud up a somewhat steep and rocky path.

"That's true. They've already tested me and found me inedible. Spit me right out." He cast a grinning look at James, who could not fully restrain a laugh.

Emily gave Cloud a look that clearly revealed her annoyance, then concentrated on leading her reluctant mount along. They seemed to be going to a great deal of difficulty simply to find a place to rest. Emily decided it might be best not to ask why, if only because she was sure she would not be calmed by the answer.

Once at the cave, Cloud and James thoroughly inspected it for animals, then ceremoniously proclaimed it bear-free and safe. She ignored their jests as she entered the cave. After so many weeks of travail, a bear was the least of her worries.

Chapter Seven

"**A**bout that mire you mentioned, Cloud?"

Looking up from the coffee he was brewing, and which he was trying yet again to show Emily how to make, Cloud frowned. "Indians?"

"Well"—James glanced at Emily—"yeh."

Frowning even more, Cloud absently told Emily, "Try to make it strong."

He strode to James's side at the opening to the cave. Things had remained peaceful for several hours, long enough for all of them to get a little sleep. Cloud supposed he should be thankful for that bit of luck. Nevertheless, what he saw below them made him curse their seemingly dismal luck, a luck that seemed to worsen each step of the way.

"Renegades," he hissed.

"Looks it. A nasty mix of outlaws and outcasts."

"Murdering bastards with no morals and less mercy. They know we're up here."

"I think I would've preferred a horde of Indians, bows taut and warpaint on."

"Yeh." Cloud cursed softly. "At least then we'd have known what we were dealing with."

"Think we can hold them off from up here?"

"We've got a strong defensive point, but they've got more men."

Knowing Cloud was merely thinking aloud, James continued in the same tone. "Each of them has to come straight into our line of fire."

"Night will be the worst time."

"So we try to drive them off before the sun goes down."

"We've been together too long, James. Save two bullets no matter what," he said softly.

Looking back at Emily and Thornton for a moment, James sighed and then looked at Cloud. "For them."

It was impossible to say the words so Cloud simply nodded, then said through clenched teeth, "I'll do the same."

A little surprised to perceive strong emotion in a man who had never displayed it before, James spoke softly and somewhat gently. "It'll hurt them a lot less and you know it. Just keep remembering what that scum'd do to them." Cloud nodded and James, knowing his own reluctance to even think of what they might have to do, grimaced. "I'll do the same."

Emily finally stood up and moved towards the two men. She did not really need to see their frowning faces to know that whatever was out there pleased them very little. It was clear to read in their taut posture and the checking of their guns. Without a word, she knelt between them and looked out, frowning when she did not see what she had expected to.

"Those are not Indians." There was the lilt of a question to her voice for she thought some of the men below did bear some resemblance to Indians.

"Some of them are."

"I thought perhaps they were. They are nothing to do with the Indians who snatched Thornton, are they, Cloud?"

"Nope. These are renegades."

"Not friends."

Deciding that she might as well know the full truth, Cloud solemnly nodded agreement. "I doubt they're friends to anybody, even each other. The Indians with them have been tossed out of their tribes and that doesn't usually happen for a small crime. There's some that are a mix of Indian and white and take the worst of both races. The whites are outlaws, probably with more than one noose waiting for them somewhere. I can see a

Mexican or two as well. And deserters, too, judging by the ragged uniforms."

"You make them sound far worse than the rest."

"Personal prejudice. Deserters killed my parents back in Arkansas near the end of the war.

"Em, what we've got down there is refuse. No one wants 'em. No one likes 'em. It's all mutual, too. They hate everybody and wouldn't blink over stealing from their own mothers—or worse. The only thing that holds them together is that, united, they might not get hanged so quick. To put it plain, honey, you think of anything evil that you can and they've done it or soon will."

She shivered. "And they've found us."

"Near to. They certainly know someone's up here. Can't say for certain if they know how many or who. If they don't, that's in our favor."

"I am able to handle a gun, Cloud."

"That may be, but you'll stay out of the way."

"I could be of some assistance."

"Em, the best help you can give me is to stay out of the way. Get Thornton and find some cover, out of sight. Oh, hell, and put out that fire. If they get much closer, they'll sniff us out."

She hurried to obey his order. It was doubtful that it would stop the renegades from finding them, but she was willing to try even the smallest chance. Once the fire was out, she hurried to get herself and Thornton out of the way.

Using the horses and their supplies, Emily built a small barricade. She convinced James and Cloud to do the same for, although the cave was safety of a sort, they would have to expose themselves occasionally to battle the renegades.

Sitting behind her makeshift barricade, Emily held Thornton close, advising him sternly not to make a sound. The men remained tensely waiting for the confrontation that was sure to come. She knew Cloud and James were admirable soldiers, but she feared for their lives. The odds were heavily weighted against them.

Seeing Cloud's saddlebags, she set Thornton aside and moved to open them. Keeping an eye on Cloud in hopes that he would not see what she was up to, she stealthily removed a pistol he had brought along to give to his brother as a gift and the box of ammunition to go with it. Quickly she sat back down next to Thornton and calmly loaded the pistol.

Cloud had clearly not believed her claim that she could handle a gun. It did not surprise her that he would be so skeptical even though she had never made any false claims before. She was able to do so little, was so utterly helpless and incompetent out in the wilderness, that it was quite natural for him to doubt her. With all her heart she prayed she would not have to prove her claim, but she was ready to do so if the need arose. Setting the pistol in her lap, she sat tensely watching the men, sharing their taut anticipiation.

When one of the renegades suddenly gave a soft cry of surprise and pointed right at them, Cloud cursed viciously. He had hoped, against all odds, that the men would give up before they found them. Rechecking his pistol and assuring himself that his rifle was readied, Cloud waited. There were several ways the men could turn now. He just hoped they made all the wrong choices.

"Since they know where we are, why're we waiting?"

"So we can be sure every shot counts," Cloud replied in a cold, flat voice.

James nodded solemnly. "How do you think they'll come at us?"

"I'm hoping straight on."

"Do you recognize this lot?"

"Nope. Most of the ones I knew much about are dead now."

"Unfortunately, there always seem to be more to take their place. They're starting up—straight at us but careful."

"There's not enough cover for them to be careful enough."

Emily had to bite her lip to keep from crying out when the first shot was fired. She held Thornton close, giving him the added protection of her body. She kept her gaze fixed upon Cloud and James and prayed as hard as she could.

The violence she was discovering in the West appalled her. It was far more visible and seemed to be more a part of everyday life than in Boston, a continually growing city that was not without its violent places and people. She could only hope that, if they got out of this confrontation alive, her brother's home and the town he lived in would not prove to be as wild and dangerous.

The shooting seemed to go on for hours, but Emily felt sure her mind exaggerated the length of the battle. Her eyes hurt from staring so fixedly at Cloud. She felt a pang of guilt over her neglect of James, who was in equal danger, but knew that, if the battle started up again, she would do the same. Although she would grieve if anything happened to James, the thought of any harm coming to Cloud made fear grip her by the throat. When it came down to the line, he was far more important to her.

"Is it Injuns, Mama?"

She forced a smile to her lips and kissed Thornton's forehead. "No, my sweet boy, not really. It is just a lot of bad men."

"Uncle Cloud and Uncle James'll make 'em go away." He patted her hand. "Don't you be afraid."

"How could I be afraid with three brave men to protect me?" Her smile came more naturally when the little boy's thin chest puffed out with pride. "We will just sit here and be quiet and soon it will be over." She hugged him when he nodded, then turned her attention back to Cloud wishing she was near enough to hear what he and James so intently discussed.

"One round finished. Think that'll be the end of it?" James began to recount his supply of ammunition.

After studying the group of renegades for a moment, Cloud shook his head and cursed softly. "Nope. They're either real stupid or real stubborn. 'Course, when you don't care squat for anybody, it's easy to throw lives away through sheer pigheadedness."

"Even though they don't know if we've got anything worth dying for or not?"

Forcing himself not to glance at Emily, Cloud sighed. "We don't know that. One of them could've spotted us. Could've seen that we had some fine horseflesh, a cart full of goods—and one woman." He nodded when James cursed. "Emily'd bring a fine purse from any number of sources."

"And if they saw her when she didn't have her bonnet on. . . ." James shook his head.

"Some don in Mexico'd pay a king's ransom for a woman with hair like that."

"And there's plenty of unscrupulous bastards between here and the border that'd buy her quick too. Here, look, one of 'em is approaching slow with a flag of truce." He watched the man edging towards them, a dirty white handkerchief tied to a stick.

"We know who's in there," the man called.

"That's odd. I don't recollect you," Cloud replied, "but then, I try to avoid scum."

Emily gasped softly over that inflammatory remark. The man clearly wished to negotiate. It seemed unwise to slap him in the face before he had even uttered his terms. She said nothing, however. Her ignorance of the area and the people in it had been well displayed more times than she cared to recall. She would be silent and assume that Cloud knew what he was doing. He had so far, bringing them safely through an area littered with dangers.

"That ain't real smart, mister. We know there's only two men, one brat, and a woman in there."

After cursing viciously under his breath, Cloud muttered, "They did see us. How the hell did I miss them?"

"You ain't got a chance."

"We haven't been doing so bad. Looks to me like you've got four, five men dead or wounded and we're still here."

"You won't be much longer. We can keep you pinned down in there for days if we have to. Look, send out the woman and we'll let you two and the brat leave safely."

"He really thinks I'm that stupid?"

"Cloud?" Emily called softly.

"Nope."

"I have not said anything yet."

"You don't have to, Em. I know what you're going to say. The answer's no."

"But, Cloud . . ."

"Em, do you have any idea what they'll do to you?"

"I'm sure it will be most unpleasant." She grimaced over her choice of words but could think of none stronger.

"Oh, yeh, most unpleasant."

Cloud cursed when he saw her flush. There was no need to sneer at her. She could have no way of knowing what sort of men they were dealing with. He was feeling frustrated, backed into a corner, but it was not fair to lash out at her. He doubted that telling her all they would do to her would stop her from wishing to save them, but he would try to make her see more clearly exactly what sort of men they were dealing with and just how little their word meant.

"Em, if you go with them, you might get lucky and the man they mean to sell you to will have a few rules about not abusing the merchandise before it gets to him. 'Course, that don't mean that scum'll follow the rules. Most likely they'll use you, repeatedly, until they kill you or find someone who'll pay a little for you. Each one of 'em, any time they want and any way they want, will have you.

"And it won't save us, Em," he continued quietly. "They'll still kill us. They won't want us on their trail and they won't want us telling anyone about them. Not only are they probably wanted in every town between here and the border, but folk out here don't take kindly to the stealing, abusing, and selling of women. If for no other reason, there's too damn few of you."

"Well, for most of us anyway," James murmured, smiling faintly when Emily gave a soft, nervous laugh. "He's right, Em. There's no dealing with this lot. They're just hoping we're fool enough to think there is."

She knew they told her the truth. It had been but a small hope, a faint chance to keep Cloud, Thornton, and James alive. Any price she had to pay would have been worth it. However, she had no inclination to toss herself to the wolves if it gained nothing. She would rather die with the people she cared for then see them cut down as she was dragged off.

"Well, it was just a thought." She hugged Thornton a little closer. "No mercy at all?"

"I'm afraid so." Glancing at the wide-eyed little boy, Cloud sorely wished he could tell her otherwise. "So, we'll show none to them."

The coldness in his voice made her shiver. This was the Cloud who had faced death and learned how to treat those who would deal it out, first in the war and then as a scout. He would do all he could to keep them alive. It would be ungrateful to quibble over the methods he employed to do that or what dark side of his character had to be called forth. Looking down at the little boy huddled so close to her, she decided she did not really care how Cloud did it, so long as he succeeded.

"You decided yet?"

"Yeh." Cloud forced back the urge to simply shoot the outlaw in answer to his loathsome offer.

"Well? What's your answer then?"

"Nope."

"She must be damned good if you're willing to die for her."

"Who says we'll be the ones doing the dying?"

"You ain't got a chance in hell."

Cloud knew James was watching the outlaw as he scrambled back to the others, so he covertly watched Emily. The way she held Thornton, talking softly and calmly to the frightened boy, touched him in a way he did not fully understand. He doubted that any mother could share a stronger bond with a child than Emily did with Thornton. It was not only sympathy and a liking for the orphaned child that would make Cloud take Thornton on. Cloud knew he would never get Emily unless he did.

"Cloud?"

"Yeh, Em?"

"If this goes—well, wrong will anyone ever know what happened to us?"

"I can't say for certain." He scowled as he suddenly realized why she would concern herself about such a thing. "Worried about Harper?"

Although puzzled by the sharp tone of his voice, she replied calmly, "Yes, he is expecting me. I would hate to think that my brother might be left with no knowledge about what has happened, or think that I have simply disappeared between Boston and his home. I have seen how that can be on a person. Sailors leave port never to return. Their loved ones know, yet do not know what has happened to them. It is assumed that the ship sank with all hands lost, yet no one saw it, no one can tell them the fate of their loved one, and there is no body. There is no real sense of finality."

Cloud opened his mouth to say something comforting, then snapped it shut as he stared at her for a moment. He carefully rethought what she had just said but did not fully trust his hearing. He had not been listening that closely.

"Your what?"

"Pardon?"

"You said that who will never know?"

"Harper."

"What did you just call him?"

"My brother." She wondered what he was getting so angry about.

"You never told me he was your brother."

She looked at Cloud in slight surprise and wondered, a little crossly, if he was quite right in the head. They were trapped in a cave with a score of ruthless desperados eager to slaughter them. It was a very strange time to get into a huff over her neglecting to mention that Harper was her brother, especially when he had made it rather clear that he was not interested in Harper in the least.

"I certainly would not be traipsing across thousands of miles to go to a stranger."

"Thought he might be your fiancé or something."

"My fiancé?" she squeaked. "Whatever gave you that idea?"

Before he could reply, James suddenly stopped grinning over the impending argument and murmured, "Here they come."

Even as he hastily turned all his attention back to the renegades, Cloud grumbled, "We'll discuss this later."

The first shot erased all thought of Harper and Cloud's strange behavior from Emily's mind. One of the desperados got in some lucky shots straight through the mouth of the cave. He was clearly not aiming for the men, but for what he felt was the reason the men were fighting so doggedly. Emily covered Thornton with her body as bullets struck the wall of the cave and they were showered with rock chips. She cast a wary glance up at the roof of the cave and prayed that it was sturdy.

Despite her need to protect Thornton, she kept a close watch on Cloud and James. They were the ones the outlaws really wished dead, the ones who were directly facing all the danger. They were also all that stood between her and what truly would be a fate worse than death for her, and for Thornton, if he were lucky, a quick death.

Thornton began to tremble and she knew all of the fears that woke him in the middle of the night were being drawn out by the battle. There were shots and the occasional scream of a man wounded or dying. All that was lacking was the continuous noise of victorious Indians, although the renegades did not fight quietly. She tried to soothe the child by word and touch but felt sure she was not doing too well. All of her own fears and memories were being roused. It was only by gritting her teeth that she kept herself from trembling right along with Thornton.

Along with never having to ride a horse again, Emily decided she never wanted to hear another gun fired. It was a foolish wish and she knew it, wincing as another bullet hit the cave wall near her, some of the stone chips hitting her, but she wished it anyway.

"They're rushing us, the bastards."

Hearing James's harsh cry, Emily quickly pushed Thornton down flat upon the floor. "Stay there, love, no matter what happens around you. Lie still and be very quiet."

"No angels, no angels."

His soft cry struck at her heart. It was evident that, in some way, Thornton did understand the things that had happened to him and were still happening. He had learned the hard lessons of death and danger. She bent to kiss the top of his head and prayed that, if he had to learn anything else this time, it was that the wrongdoers did not always win.

"Quiet now, Thornton. We can all fight better if we know you're doing as you should." She saw him nod and turned her attention back to James and Cloud just in time to see the renegades appear in the mouth of the cave as they rushed forward.

The last clear thought Emily had was that the renegades plainly cared as little for each other's lives as they did for their victims'. It was nearly suicidal to rush such rapidly firing men in a strong defensive position. Then the first renegade broke through the mouth of the cave, and she took up the pistol she had readied. Although her stomach clenched and heaved, the violence played out before her making her ill, she was ready to do her part to help Cloud if help was needed.

Cloud used every trick and skill he had ever acquired to fight back the rush of men. Only the relative lack of space in the cave's opening kept them from being overwhelmed. It also helped that, although seeming to charge recklessly, the renegades tried to maintain some caution. That brief reluctance to hurl themselves into the line of fire kept the numbers coming at him and James manageable. Cloud doggedly continued to fight while praying, for the first time in a long time, that no sudden surge of men would come to bury them.

He also fought to bury a fear that knotted his insides, a fear for the safety of Emily and Thornton. It was far from the first time he had been responsible for other lives, women and children as well as men, but never had he found it so difficult to put all thought of them aside and concentrate on beating the enemy. He could not shake the image of the two helpless innocents huddled in the rear of the cave or of what would happen to them if he failed them.

Then, when the renegades began to hesitate, to hold back, he began to lose that fear of failure. The knot in his stomach began to loosen as he began to feel that Emily was safe.

Emily sensed a change before she actually saw it. Slowly, she began to relax as the intensity of the fighting eased. She forced herself not to think of the deaths they had caused and sternly reminded herself that those men had intended to kill them.

Just as she was about to check on Thornton, slipping the pistol into the pocket of her skirt, a hand covered her mouth. She tried to cry out despite the dirty gag, but an arm about her throat cut off her air. Her struggles were fruitless as she tried to stop herself from being dragged backwards. Panic stung her throat as she realized that there was a back entrance to the cave and the renegades had found it. She prayed to God that James or Cloud would turn around but they never did and were still facing away from her as she lost sight of them. She wondered frantically if she would ever see them again as her loss of air finally caused her to black out.

"Hey, look! The bastards are hightailing it. We did it, Cloud! We did it." James slapped Cloud on the back.

Smiling with relief, Cloud turned to tell

Emily it was over, but his smile quickly vanished. Bolting to the back of the cave, he found only a shaking Thornton still pressed to the floor. It was another moment of frantic searching before he found the crevice that led to another entrance. Frozen in place, he stared into the darkness and realized that he had won the battle but lost the war.

Chapter Eight

"**D**idn't you know there was two ways into this place?"

"No," Cloud ground out as he threw their gear together. "I never bothered to look."

"Angels took her. Angels took my mama."

"There weren't any damned angels," Cloud snarled at the weeping little child, then immediately regretted it. Crouching down by the child, Cloud said gently, "No angels, Thornton. Renegades. Bad men. Your mama's alive. We just have to find her." He handed the boy a handkerchief and Thornton began to calm a little.

"Bad men?" Thornton dutifully blew when Cloud held the handkerchief to his nose. "We can find Mama?"

"We'll find her. Now listen to me, Thornton. Listen very carefully." The boy nodded. "This won't be easy. It'll also be dangerous. You'll have to do everything I tell you to, do it exactly and without a whimper. If I set you down and tell you to stay, you stay."

"Even if it's dark?" he asked softly.

"Even if it's dark. The mule and the mare, Carolynn, will be with you most likely."

"Okay, Uncle Cloud. I'll do everything and you'll get Mama back."

Cloud nodded and tried to feel as confident as he made himself sound. If he had some safe place to leave everything so that James and he could travel light, he would have an excellent chance. Instead, he had to try and trail men who would be moving stealthily yet quickly, while he had to drag along a little boy, a stubborn mule, and a cartload of supplies. It would slow him down dangerously and he had to reach the men before they crossed the border. Once the men got Emily into Mexico, it would be a long and arduous chore to get her back. He knew neither the land nor the language.

By the time they were ready to leave, Cloud felt tied up in knots. Already half an hour had been lost. He was painfully aware of how much of a lead that could give the renegades. The fear of all that could happen to Emily during that time gnawed at him.

"Cloud?"

Struggling to shake free of his dismal

thoughts without taking his gaze from the trail they followed, Cloud muttered, "What is it, James?"

"I don't like to be the bearer of bad tidings—but a storm's brewing."

Cloud looked up at the sky and began to curse softly and viciously. James was right. A storm would slow the renegades, but it would also obliterate any trail they left. He could only pray that they were able to find Emily before that disaster occurred.

Emily was first aware of the smell of horse combined with that of a unwashed body. She nearly gagged on it as she slowly returned to consciousness. Then her memory returned and she tensed, slowly opening her eyes while dreading what she would see.

All around her rode the renegades. Some seemed badly wounded. Even as she watched, one man slid from his saddle. Another man dismounted, felt for a pulse, then pronounced the man dead. To Emily's shock and disgust, the man then stripped the body, remounted and, taking the reins of the dead man's horse, started on his way again. Emily decided that nothing else could have shown her more clearly that these men cared nothing for anyone.

No one spoke to her. She decided that was probably for the best, so she made no sound. The last thing she wanted to do was to draw any attention to herself. She did try to edge away from the odiferous man she rode with, but the arm around her waist tightened painfully whenever she moved.

She tried not to think about all that could happen to her, but her mind refused to grant her that peace. Every word Cloud had said about the renegades echoed in her mind. It was far too easy to visualize the horrors that could be facing her.

A faint hope that Cloud could save her flickered in her heart, but she struggled to douse it. There were at least a dozen renegades, although some seemed to be in poor shape. That represented odds that she dreaded to see Cloud facing. He was strong, knew the territory, and had a fighting skill even she recognized as notable, but she felt sure he would be hard-pressed with no sturdy defensive position to take up. She was terrified and dreaded what was to come, but she did not want her freedom bought at the cost of Cloud's life. Unfortunately, she could not see any way to gain that freedom for herself.

It began to grow dark, but Emily was sure it was still too early for nightfall. Glancing up at the sky, she marveled at the blackness of the clouds rolling across the sky and obliterating the sun. The sky looked malevolent and she found that fitting.

The horses began to grow restless and Emily sensed a tension growing amongst the men. It was finally decided that they would stop and try to shelter themselves in some meager way from the impending storm. She shivered as a chill entered the increasing wind and wondered just how bad a storm they were in for.

When they halted, she was roughly set down, then kept a close watch on. Even if she had been able to loosen the bonds that held her wrists behind her back she knew she would not have gotten very far. She sat down and watched as a camp was erected in the shelter of some large boulders, a camp she doubted would offer much shelter if the sky delivered the torrents of rain it seemed to promise.

As soon as everything was settled to the leader's instructions, she was leashed to a stake by a rope tied to her ankle. She was seated with her back to a large rock, sticks and a worn blanket providing a flimsy shelter. If the rains did come, she knew she would be dangerously soaked and chilled. Settling back against the rock, she listened to the men talking as they sat a few feet away around the campfire. Their words frightened her, but she felt she had to know it all.

"Why can't we do nothing with her, Burt? Ain't seen such a fine piece in a real long time."

" 'Cause I said no. You have a bit and the rest'll want some. That'd probably kill a little thing like her and a dead woman won't bring us any money, you fool. Now leave it, Bob. Corey, you set out extra guards like I told you?"

"I did, Burt. Sure it's worth it? There wasn't any sign of them following."

"Don't mean they aren't."

"You think they'd risk that much for the woman?"

"As Bob said, she's a fine piece. Women ain't that plentiful and pretty ones ain't found too easy at all."

Burt glanced her way and Emily shivered. He had the coldest eyes she had ever seen. Cloud could look cold, but she knew that, for the most part, it was simply an expression donned to hide his thoughts or feelings. Burt was hiding nothing. The coldness went to his soul. His eyes revealed his lack of humanity, of all the things that could raise a man above the beasts or, she thought with a tremor, in Burt's case, a rabid beast.

"Rodrigo will pay plenty for this one. Fair, pretty and clean."

"Burt, she ain't untouched."

"What makes you so sure, Bob?"

"Well, she was traveling with them two men and she had that kid hanging onto her skirts."

"So you figure you can have a bit."

"Well, how's Rodrigo gonna know if we do?"

"He'll know. He always does. He won't cut the price much if she ain't virgin, but he won't give us a cent if she's like the last one we brought him. He don't want her bad used or beat. You'll leave her be, Bob."

There was no threat put into the words, but Burt's voice held all the threat they needed to hear. Emily relaxed a little. She might face horror at the end of her journey, but she would not have to suffer it the whole way there. It was comfort of a sort and she tried to pull some strength from the knowledge. She knew she would need all she could muster.

Just as she started to doze off, Burt approached and crouched before her. He held out a plate of beans. Her stomach rolled with hunger, but she lifted her gaze from the food she wanted so desperately to meet Burt's steady gaze with a look of haughty disgust.

"You expect me to lick my meal from the plate?" She did not like the way his eyes widened slightly, a mercenary gleam lightening their cold depths for a moment.

"I mean to loose your hands. You ain't going nowheres." Setting down the plate, Burt did just that.

Picking up the plate, Emily said, fighting for a calm she did not feel at all, "I am not without family that will search for me."

"Let 'em search. Once Rodrigo has you, they'll never find you."

Since she suspected that was true, she had no reply and concentrated on eating the beans. She then drank the too-strong coffee he pressed upon her. The last drop had barely passed her lips when he retied her wrists behind her back. She tensed when he took a strand of her hair between his dirt-blackened fingers, studying it closely.

"Rodrigo'll pay a fortune just because of the hair," Corey said as he approached them.

"That he will. Ain't many women with such fine hair. He'll pay a lot for something else too." Burt slowly stood up.

"Yeh, she sure is a pretty little thing. Don't think we've ever grabbed ourselves a prettier one."

"Nope, don't think we have either, but that ain't it. We have us a lady—from the east."

"Yeh? Think Rodrigo'll like that?"

"Oh, yeh, he will. He'll like that fine. We're going to do well with this one." He stood up and stared at Emily for a moment longer before heading back to the campfire, Corey in tow. "Very well indeed."

Emily shivered. It seemed that, by opening her big mouth she had made herself more valuable. She wished she had kept silent. Since her value had just been raised, they would undoubtedly hold onto her even tighter. Although she was not sure she could have managed a successful escape, she sincerely doubted she would even get a chance to try for one now.

When the rain started, it seemed fitting. She was not surprised when her flimsy covering proved no protection at all. Huddling as close as she could to the rock, she tried to make herself as small as possible in a vain attempt to lessen the area the rain had to strike. It was going to be a long, cold, uncomfortable night.

The urge to weep swamped her, but she fought it. It would gain her nothing and, although she had no real hope to grasp at, she did not want to give in to complete despair. That would steal her wits, make her too accepting of her fate and then, if by some miracle, a chance to escape or help herself came her way, she might well be too cowed to grab at it.

Huddled against an uncomfortable rock, cold and wet, she lacked the strength to keep her thoughts from Cloud. There was, however, comfort to be found in the knowledge that he, James, and Thornton were alive. She just prayed that Cloud felt no inclination to be gallant and try to come after her, thus putting the three of them right back into a perilous situation.

Cloud rode ahead of James, leaving Thornton with his friend. While James tried to secure some sort of shelter for them from the threatening storm he intended to scout ahead. If nothing else, he thought morosely, he could at least assure himself of the direction the renegades were headed before the storm obliterated the trail.

Just as the rain began, telling Cloud that his time was up, he heard the sound of a horse made nervous by the storm. His heart tightened with hope as he quickly secured his mount out of sight. Stealthily, he moved toward the sound. Despite being soaked with a cold, steady rain, he was suddenly glad of the inclement weather. Instinct told him he had found the place the renegades had stopped to wait out the storm. The rain, clouds, and wind cut visibility and disguised noises, both of which could only aid him.

When he saw the man, Cloud smiled coldly. The renegade was huddled in his poncho, most of his attention taken up by a vain attempt to stay warm and dry. If the other guards were that careless, Cloud felt sure that he and James would have little trouble disposing of them. Cautiously, he retreated after carefully noting where the man was placed. He would circle the camp, which he judged to be within a barely visible circle of rocks, and locate any other guards before he returned to James to plan and execute Emily's rescue, a rescue he began to feel was well within his grasp.

James swiftly drew his pistol when a rider suddenly appeared from out of the driving rain. "Hold it right there."

"It's me, James."

"Christ, Cloud, where the hell've you been? I began to think the impossible had finally happened, that you'd got lost."

After securing his horse, Cloud crawled beneath the cart where James and Thornton huddled. "This the best you could do?"

"You expected a two-room cabin with a fireplace?" James became aware of the tension in Cloud almost immediately. "You've found the bastards, haven't you."

"I have. If we hadn't stopped here, we would've rolled right into them. They're that close."

"You found Mama?"

"I found her, Thornton, but I don't have her yet. That'll take a little time and work."

"Only a little?" James muttered. "Well, let's have it. I assume you have some sort of plan."

"First we silence the guards."

"How many?"

"Four and only one of them seems alert. The others were more concerned with staying dry or as dry as they could. They probably think the storm'll halt all pursuit."

"Did you see Em?"

"Nope. Saw the fire of the camp though. I know where she is. Didn't want to chance discovery."

" 'Course not. We can reconnoiter after we've disposed of the guards. It'll be safer that way. How many do you think are left?"

"Take away four guards, and that'll leave us with a manageable number."

"Yeh, if we get Em out of the line of fire. Can't let them use her to hide behind. So, once we get rid of the guards, we'll meet back at the point where we first separated and approach the camp together.

"Good. What about Thornton?"

"He stays here." Cloud looked at the boy. "You understand, Thornton? You wait right here no matter what. If I'm to have a chance of getting your mother back, I can't be worrying about you. I certainly can't take you with me because we've got to be real quiet and move quickly, and there'll be some fighting. I want to know you'll be setting right here where you've been left."

"I will, Uncle Cloud. I won't move an inch 'til you bring my mama back. I can set still real good."

"That's a brave fellow." He ruffled the boy's damp hair. "That's as important to saving your mother as anything James and I can do. Ready, James?"

"I'm ready. Just point out my quarry."

"With pleasure."

When they reached the point where Cloud had first heard the guard's horse, they separated. Cloud gave James detailed directions on the two guards he was to silence, as well as what information he had gathered in his brief observation of them. As soon as James had disappeared Cloud began to approach his quarry.

The moment the guard was in sight, Cloud pulled out his knife. For once he knew he would feel no regret over the taking of a life. He had always considered renegades a scourge, and this time they had touched him personally. As Cloud stalked the man, waiting for the best time to strike, he decided he was doing the world no small favor in ridding it of such men.

It was several moments before the man stood still in a position that would allow Cloud to spring from his hiding place unseen. He wanted no outcry, no matter how small. In one swift move, he clamped his hand over the man's mouth, snapped the man's head back and drew his knife over the renegade's vulnerable throat. In the past he had always felt remorse and disgust for being brought to such a pass, but neither touched him now. Before the man had finished falling to the ground, Cloud was stealthily moving on to the next guard.

Removing the second guard took a little longer. Cloud wondered if the man sensed something, for he was overly restless. When he finally got the chance to move, however, Cloud did so quickly, quietly, and efficiently. As he trotted back to the meeting place, he hoped that James had been as fortunate.

Cloud was kept waiting several long, nerve-wracking minutes before James wandered back and muttered, "Quick, aren't you. No trouble?"

"None. And you?"

"Just the tedium of waiting for my chance. Our route of retreat is clear. Now for Emily."

"Now for Emily and, I think, it'd be wise to make sure that no one is left to chase after us."

James nodded and sighed. "That'd probably be best. Losing so many men might not be deterrent enough."

"Nope. Might even make them vengeful, even if they didn't care squat for any of the ones that died."

They crept towards the camp as stealthily as their considerable skill allowed despite the noise of the storm. Cloud spotted Emily and signaled James to halt. Lying on their bellies on the increasingly muddy ground, they both studied the camp.

"Perfect. Em is separated from the rest," Cloud whispered. "You keep watch from up here while I circle round behind her and cut her free. Don't shoot too soon but don't let any of them start toward her. They'd just as soon kill her as let us get her free."

"Right. Take care," he called softly as Cloud started to edge towards Emily.

Keeping his gaze fixed upon Emily and trusting James to watch the renegades, Cloud slinked towards her. She looked miserable, cold, and wet but there was no sign that she had been abused in any way. He felt hope rise that he had been right, that the renegades saw how much greater her value was if she remained relatively unharmed. He wished he could let her know in some way that he was coming for her, so that she would not give him away when he first reached her, but he knew such a thing could prove fatal. He could only hope that she still had the wit to control and hide any surprise she felt.

Emily sighed as she finally accepted the fact that she would never get to sleep. It was not only her extreme discomfort that kept her from finding the ease of that oblivion, but fear. All her efforts to still her fear had failed and it was a living thing within her. She could taste it, nearly smell it. Closing her eyes only gave visual strength to her fears as her mind worked against her.

Shifting her position a little, she tensed. She could feel the pistol in her pocket and was stunned that she could have forgotten such a thing—or that her captors had not searched for a weapon. She reasoned that her skirts were voluminous enough to hide its bulk and that the renegades simply did not think a woman like her would either have a weapon or use it against them if she did. Emily heartily wished she could get free, so that she could show them just how wrong they were.

A strong shiver tore through her and she wished she could free her hands, simply so that she could wrap her arms about herself. Just as she was thinking, somewhat darkly, that it would serve the renegades right if she died of pneumonia, she felt a tug on the ropes that bound her wrists. Slowly she tensed, thinking that it could be someone helping her, but that it could also be one of the renegades up to something that would be of no benefit to her whatsoever. She was too afraid of disappointment to hope for the former.

"Easy, Em." Cloud spoke as softly as he could yet still be heard by Emily. "Don't draw their attention, honey. Be still."

Cloud! her mind screamed in relief as she grew so still that she nearly forgot to breathe. Her heart felt as if it had climbed into her throat. She was both exhilarated over the thought of regaining her freedom and terrified for Cloud.

He could feel her trembling and was not sure if it was simply from the cold. "Even when you feel the ropes loosen, don't move. Sit as if you're still tied. When I tell you to, try to move your body so I can get some cover behind it while I cut your ankle free."

When he breathed the signal, she turned slightly onto her side facing the renegades. It was not easy to leave her arms as they had been without rubbing her aching wrists or using her hands to help herself move. So too was it hard not to see Cloud, to judge his presence only by a whisper in the dark. If her wrists had not been freed she might have feared that her mind was slipping, making her imagine what was not there. Then a gentle, calloused hand briefly stroked her rope-burned ankle and that made her fears ease.

"Now, darlin', try to act as if you're still

bound, keep your eyes on that scum and start to edge back this way."

She shook with the effort and her eyes stung from staring fixedly at the renegades, but she did not falter as she followed his directions, his whispered encouragement giving her strength. As soon as she reached the outer edge of the rock she had been huddled against, a strong arm curled around her waist and she was yanked behind the rock. Silently, Cloud pushed and dragged her along, but they were only a few feet away when an outcry was raised. Emily gasped as the air seemed to be suddenly filled with the sound of gunfire.

Although her body seemed loathe to work with the slightest semblance of coordination, Emily fought to move as fast as Cloud urged her to. Suddenly he shoved her down on the ground. A bullet skidded into the ground only inches from her nose.

"Where the hell did he come from?" Cloud grumbled as he raised his pistol, only to swear viciously when it misfired.

Glancing up, Emily saw the renegade smile, thinking he had them trapped. Without thought, she pulled the pistol from her pocket, raised herself up on one knee, extended her right arm out straight and fired. The renegade stood there for an instant longer, staring in horrified wonder at the hole in his chest—then collapsed.

"Where the hell did you get that?"

"Your saddlebags." She wondered why her

voice sounded so high and unnatural. "I told you I could shoot."

"Fine. You can." He snatched the gun from her, then gently pushed her to start her moving again. "You won't do it again. Not at a man, if I can help it."

"I rather hope you can," she whispered, then forced her shocked senses to concentrate on escape and escape alone. She did not even complain when, once they were on level ground, Cloud picked her up, flung her over his shoulder and started to run. The gunfire soon stopped and shortly afterwards James fell into step behind them.

She was still dazed when Cloud set her down, then urged her to crawl beneath the cart. He quickly wrapped a slightly damp blanket around her. She sat still, not sure she should believe that she was really safe again, but then Thornton flung himself into her arms and clung tightly. His compact little body was all the proof she needed. Lying down with the boy still in her arms she looked at Cloud, who scrunched down at her side.

"They are all dead, aren't they."

"It had to be that way, Em. I'll admit there's always a touch of vengence in it for me."

"Because of your parents."

"Yeh." He gently stroked her forehead. "They were butchered, everything was taken, and the farm was burned down. My sister Skye was nearly burned alive in it. She was

148

hiding in the root cellar. I never did find all the men who did it."

"And one of these might have been one."

"Slim chance, but the thought's always there. Come on, enough talk. You need to rest."

"I know. Thank you."

"My pleasure. Now, shut up and go to sleep."

Smiling faintly she reached over Thornton to take Cloud's hand, then closed her eyes. She decided she was quite mad. Cloud's 'shut up' was beginning to sound like an endearment.

Chapter Nine

"Sorry about this, Em."

Turning from her survey of the somewhat dilapitated cabin, Emily smiled faintly. "It is dry. That makes it nearly a castle."

"C'mon." He took her by the arm and tugged her into the second and smallest of the two rooms. "You've got to get out of those wet clothes. You're shivering." He set her bag down on the dusty bed. "I'll get Thornton seen to, then we can clean up a bit. We can afford to rest here for a spell."

She nodded and he left her alone. Although the damp buttons gave her chilled fingers some trouble, she was soon out of her clothes. The rain had finally stopped, but there had been no sun to dry her and she felt as if she had been wet for weeks instead of just a night and a day. Fortunately, her bag had been well protected in the cart, so her spare clothes were more or less dry and she sighed with relief as she donned them.

The only thing that remained to trouble her was the way Cloud was acting. He was solicitous but somewhat aloof. Not a word had been said concerning her time, thankfully brief as it was, with the renegades. She had the unsettling feeling that Cloud might think more happened to her while she was there than really had, but she was not sure how to initiate a talk about the matter to clear up any misconceptions.

Shaking her head, she decided to wait until they were alone. Perhaps, as they lay alone in the dark, she would find both courage and inspiration. For now, she decided as she frowned at the dusty bed, she would busy her body and her fretful mind with the chore of cleaning. There was certainly more than enough of that to do.

It was growing dark before they all collapsed at the now scrubbed table in the main room. Looking around, Emily decided that the air of disuse and the layers of dust had made the cabin look far worse than it was. It was still showing signs of age and disrepair, but she now had no objections at all to staying in it.

"Do you know who used to live here?" she asked Cloud and hoped no one would hear the way her stomach was growling in response to the aroma of James's rabbit stew.

"A fur trapper name of Josh Tucker. He's been dead for nigh on five years. The cabin's become a traveler's haven."

"Maybe we ought to do a little work around here or the next traveler might find his haven falling down around his ears," James murmured as he set a pot of coffee on the table. "Either no one has been here for a while or they just used the place and left. Some people don't understand the unwritten laws out here."

Emily nodded as she helped herself to some of the strong coffee, savoring the way it warmed her. It was a drink she had had little of back home, but she was quickly becoming used to it. She doubted, however, that she would ever learn to make it to Cloud's satisfaction.

During the meal, Emily found herself a little concerned about Thornton. His usually hearty appetite seemed dimmed and he was uncustomarily quiet. Thornton claimed only tiredness, however, and bolstered that claim by immediately seeking his bed, a pallet made up on the floor next to the cot where James intended to sleep. Cloud and James further eased her worries by stressing that even a lively boy like Thornton would be worn out by all they had been through in the last twenty-four hours.

For a while she struggled to stay awake with the men but soon felt too weary to do so. It troubled her a little that Cloud simply bade her good-night when she said she was going to turn in. As she got ready for bed, she scolded herself for looking for trouble where it did not exist, but it did little to ease her worry. It had been several days since they made love and, while this could easily be due to the rigors and lack of privacy on the trail, she began to fear that Cloud was tired of her. As she crawled into bed, she hoped he would soon join her to dispel those fears.

"Might I ask why you're honoring me with your company instead of following pretty little Emily?"

Cloud glanced at James, then stared into the flames of the fire they sat in front of. "Em needs to rest, and if I crawl in with her before she gets to sleep, I won't let her get much of that—at least not right away." He scowled. "I'd want to try and erase all memory of those bastards."

"Do you think they touched her?"

The mere thought of such a thing twisted Cloud's insides into knots. "I don't think so, but then I keep thinking why shouldn't they?"

"True. I doubt they've had anything as fine as Em fall into their hands before, Yet, she doesn't act as if she was—well, abused."

"Nope, but would she if she had been? Em

can hide a lot behind her lady's training and stiff Yankee pride. I've got a feeling that a shame like rape would be something she'd do her best to hide."

"Or, she wasn't raped. She was badly frightened, though, and she might just be wishing you'd come and keep her awake for a while, comfort her and ease those fears she now carries. There's something else, too, that's sure to be troubling her. She shot a man."

"Hell, yeh. I still can't believe that."

"She said she could shoot."

"Yeh, and she's no liar, but she's so damned helpless out here I found it hard to believe."

"Well, that's got to be preying on her even though I think she is smart enough to know that it was necessary, that she had no choice."

"True. Well,"—Cloud stood up—"you've convinced me. I might not gain much by joining her but I'll lose a lot if I don't. 'Night, James."

"Get her to tell you what happened, Cloud."

"I intend to. You'll secure the place for the night?"

"I will. Get to bed."

Cloud cautiously entered the other room and silently shut the door behind him. Although Emily was in bed and lying still, he sensed that she was still awake. There was too much tension in her body. He sincerely hoped that was not due to him, to the fact that he would soon crawl in beside her, as he moved to undress and wash up before getting into bed.

He felt uncertain and that annoyed him a little, but he forced himself to accept it. Women's moods and feelings had never been of any great concern to him. His reaction to a display of them had simply been to walk away. That was something he could not do this time, although he felt himself tempted. As he slipped into bed beside her, he hoped he did not end up with his foot planted firmly in his mouth.

Emily tried to relax when he gently tugged her into his arms. She had tried to go to sleep, but it had proven fruitless. The greatest deterrent had been the memory of shooting the renegade. Every time she closed her eyes, she saw it all too clearly and, now that the danger was not immediate, she found it hard to justify. So too was she beset with worries about Cloud and the odd way he was treating her. Even now, as he held her, she sensed a holding back, a reserve.

"You should be asleep, Em."

"I tried. I think it is going to prove impossible."

"Because of what those men did to you?" he asked gently, trying to hide the sudden tension he felt over the possibility of hearing something he did not really want to hear.

"No," she answered softly, "because of what I had to do. Oh, God, Cloud!" She covered her face with her hands as she started to weep. "I killed a man. I can see him whenever I close my eyes. I can see how he looked and see the blood."

"Em, sweetheart." He tugged her hands away and kissed her cheeks. "He was set to blow my head off."

"So delicately put." She could not fully repress a smile, but it faltered quickly. "I keep telling myself that, but it does little good. I have never shot a person before, just targets and a bird once."

"Only once?"

"Well, yes. I didn't really like it, although I had been taught to shoot in order to join my family on the fall hunt. Still, I had trouble stomaching it, for birds are such harmless creatures and none of us needed them for food. We had plenty."

"So you learned to shoot with a rifle."

She nodded. "The lad teaching me taught me a pistol as well, although it was not suggested that he do so. I wish he hadn't taught me," she whispered.

"Well, I'm damn glad he did or I'd be dead and you'd be a prisoner again."

"Of course. I'm not thinking straight. I must try to remember that."

"And remember what they planned to do to you." He saw her wince and felt her shiver. "Em, what did they do to you?"

"Nothing really." She saw him frown slightly with a hint of disbelief. "Truly. It seems I was of more value untouched."

"I'd wondered if that could be the case, but I still feel you're damned lucky it was that way."

"I realize that. There was one man who made it very clear what he would prefer doing, but the man that seemed to be the leader, a man named Burt, convinced him otherwise. A man named Rodrigo was the one they were taking me to. From what was said I gather they have brought him some sadly abused women in the past. Rodrigo made some rules and Burt meant for them to be followed, for he felt I could bring him a lot of money."

"Yeh, you would've, honey." He caressed her hair. "This hair was nothing less than gold in that bastard's hands. Some Mexican don'd pay more than old Burt's probably ever seen. It must've sorely tried him to leave you alone, but greed proved stronger than lust, thank God."

"He also heard, in the way I spoke, that I was from the east."

"And a well-bred, probably educated lady to boot. He must've felt his bag of coins growing nearly too heavy to carry."

"I know these men are dead and will threaten no one again, but others will take their places, won't they?"

"I'm afraid so, darlin'. A few more rocks'll

be turned over and more just like them'll crawl out to plague the territory."

"And steal women from their homes and families to be sold like cattle. Can nothing be done?"

"Not too much, I'm afraid. Just stop 'em when you can. This area needs more settlers, more towns, and more laws. That'll make it a lot harder, but I'm not real sure you can ever stop that sort of thing completely. But there's no use fretting on it, little one. Just be glad that you're not added to that sad number and that some of that scum's gone for good."

She wrapped her arms around him and pressed her cheek against his chest. "I am and I will keep reminding myself of that. I am finding it hard to—well, to adjust to the violence, the wildness, of this West of yours."

"There's violence in the east."

"True, but it's the shadowy sort and a lot of people can live their whole lives and have but the barest knowledge of it around them. Do you think it will be a little less rowdy where Harper is?"

"A lot less rowdy. And speaking of Harper . . ." He put one finger beneath her chin and urged her to look up at him.

She eyed him a little warily when she saw his frown. "What about Harper?"

"You didn't tell me he was your brother."

"I'm sure I did."

"Nope. You never said anything that'd lead

159

me to think he was kin."

"The simple fact that I was traveling hundreds of miles on the strength of an inviting letter should have told you something."

"Yeh, that you had strong feelings for the fellow, which could make him a lot of things besides a brother."

"If I had had a fiancé or a husband, I would have waved them under your nose to try and deter you from the deal we made."

She wondered if he would now confess to his trickery, but she was not surprised when he did not. Confessing to such a thing would not gain him very much, could even cause him a great deal of trouble. If she had such a trick to confess, she would find it very hard to admit to. She did wonder, however, if he would ever honor her with the truth. It was hard to believe that he really wished to be seen as a heartless rogue who would desert a woman and small child in desperate straits unless he got some kind of compensation for it.

Cloud felt what was now the habitual pinch of guilt over his deception, but he pushed it aside. "It wouldn't have mattered."

"Not at all?"

"Nope."

"And what matters now?"

"What do you mean?"

Staring at her hand as she smoothed it over his broad chest, she said quietly, "You have treated me differently since the rescue.''

"Ah, Em.'' He held her tightly. "I didn't know what you may have suffered and I didn't know what to say or do if you had been used badly. I was feeling damned guilty too.''

"About what? You rescued me. That is hardly something to feel guilty about.''

"I chose that cave for our shelter. I should've looked it over more carefully, should've known about the other way in. I've been soldiering and scouting for near to ten years. I should've had a good look out of sheer habit.''

For a while they simply held each other. Emily felt her lingering fears smoothed away by his stroking hands. She soon felt his passion begin to conquer his sympathy, however. Smiling faintly, she felt her own desires begin to respond to that and knew she was going to recover from her ordeal just fine, that the fears it had inspired could be set aside.

"Harper Brockinger. Of course.''

Emily looked up at him as he suddenly urged her onto her back. "You know him?''

"Does he live in a town called Lockridge in the San Luis Valley?''

"Why, yes, he does. He and his wife, Dorothy.''

"Owns a store.''

"You do know him.''

"Vaguely.''

"Then you must know just where Lockridge is."

"Oh, yeh, I know where it is. My brother's ranch and my piece of land sit just outside of it."

"Well, that is a surprising coincidence." Surprising but not necessarily good, she thought, for it meant that he would be living very close by and, if he cast her aside as was his habit with women, that could prove to be a living hell for her. "Funny we have taken so long to see that."

"Would've seen it sooner except that I wasn't bothered with exactly where in the valley you were headed. Figured we'd just get to Wolfe's place and then sort it out."

He also knew that the names Harper and Brockinger should have come together in his mind, but he made no mention of it. She might ask him why it had not done so and he was not about to tell her that he had forced Harper from his mind because he did not like her association with some other man. That tasted of jealousy and, while he might admit to himself that that was probably just what he suffered from, he certainly did not want her guessing it.

Now, there was a whole new collection of troubles. Harper Brockinger and his wife were at the top of what the small but growing town of Lockridge considered society. They would not look kindly upon him as a suitor for Emily. He was, after all, part Indian, a fact that most of Lockridge quietly overlooked unless he got too close to them or their women. He and his brother had made their place in the town mostly by a judicious use of their fists, beating any man that openly derided them for their heritage, and the fact that they legally held and had tamed a large tract of land just outside of town. There were enough open-minded people who could accept them without prejudice to make life comfortable, but Cloud knew that Dorothy Brockinger was not one of them. He might just have to fight for Emily, not simply court her. But he felt no hesitation about that. She was well worth the trouble.

"You have gone very quiet," she said softly as she moved her hand down his side to caress his hip.

"Thinking."

"About what?"

"About making love to you."

She blushed faintly. "I have always preferred a doer to a thinker."

"Happy to oblige, ma'am," he growled as he bent his head to kiss her.

Emily swatted at the hand on her shoulder, shaking her gently. She could hear soft voices, but tried to block them out. All she wanted to do was sleep. Then a sound reached her that abruptly ended all her attempts to ignore the outside world.

"Thornton's crying," she mumbled as she sat up, clutching the sheet to her chest, and found a frowning James bending over her.

"Cloud's just gone to him, Em, but the boy wants you."

"What's wrong with him? Could you turn around, please?"

Doing so, James explained, "He says he doesn't feel well, Em. I can't get any real answers. He just wants you."

Hurriedly dressing, she asked, "Has he been vomiting or anything like that?"

"Yeh, that's why Cloud and I decided to get you. That's what really started him crying too. He's just plain miserable, poor kid."

Still buttoning up her dress, she hurried toward the door. James quickly fell into step behind her. Just as she stepped into the room, Thornton was ill again. Her stomach clenched in sympathy as Cloud held the little boy who heaved but had little left to bring up.

"I've changed my mind, James. I think Em ought to stay away from the boy." Cloud held Thornton when the boy saw Emily and tried to move towards her. "He's hot as hell. I don't want Em getting whatever it is."

"Mama," Thornton wept and reached out towards her.

Emily shook off James's gentle restraining hold and hurried towards Thornton. Ignoring Cloud's scowl, she took the child into her arms, knowing she could not have acted otherwise. It was not even necessary to feel Thornton's face to know that he had a fever; his little body was hot enough to feel uncomfortable against her. She heartily wished that she knew about illness and caring for the sick.

"I don't want you falling sick too, Em." Cloud crouched before the pair sitting on James's bed, and even as he spoke, he knew he had no chance at all of keeping Emily away from the boy.

"Perhaps I won't. I seem to be very resilient to sickness. Nevertheless, he needs me, so here I stay." She urged a quieting Thornton to lie down. "Poor little man. Let's see what we can do for you. But you must be quiet, love. Getting so upset only makes you feel worse. Now, I'm going to get some cool water and try to ease this fever you have."

Forcing down her very real fears for the boy, Emily set to work. She bathed his small body with cool water time and time again. Despite his fretful objections, she forced him to drink a lot of thin broth and weak coffee, heartily wishing that she had some good herbal tea. She became oblivious to everything else, including the hours that dragged by.

Cloud scowled toward the bed where Thornton lay, Emily smoothing a cool cloth over the boy's forehead and talking soothing nonsense to the child. "She's going to make herself sick going on like this without rest," he muttered to James, who sat at the table with him.

"Make her take some time away from his bedside then," James said.

"I've tried. He won't let her go. Poor kid's miserable and scared but, hell, she needs a break from it."

"If you can take her away from him, I can watch him for a while."

"Get ready then," Cloud muttered as he rose and strode towards Emily, "because she's taking a rest from it even if I have to drag her away by the hair." He stopped by Emily's side and took her by the arm, tugging her to her feet despite her tired protest. "James can watch the boy. You're coming with me."

"Mama!"

"Enough out of you, young man. Your mother needs to rest. She isn't going far and she'll come back. You don't want her getting sick too, do you?"

The boy shook his head, but Cloud was not sure he understood, for he was gravely ill. Cloud hurried a reluctant Emily out of the cabin before Thornton could start to call for her again. Despite her protests, he dragged Emily along until they were far enough away from the cabin that Thornton's fretful cries could not be heard.

"Cloud, he needs me," Emily said a little crossly as he pressed her to sit down beneath a tree.

"You need to rest." He sat down next to

her. "Just for a little while. Take some time
away from all his demands."

She nodded, knowing he was right, and
leaned heavily against him when he put his
arm around her shoulders. As they sat there
quietly, she felt her fears for Thornton break
free and choke her. Constant tending to him
had been enough to keep them to the back
of her mind. Now they forced her to look at
them.

"Will he die?" she asked softly.

"I don't know, Em. I just don't know."

"Oh, God, he can't die. After all he's been
through, he just can't!"

He held her close as she wept. A part of
him wished to join her, but he knew she
needed him to be strong for her. When she
finally fell into an exhausted slumber, he
closed his eyes and started praying. He
admitted that he had become inordinately
fond of the little boy, but he knew his prayers
were mostly for Emily's sake. Cloud knew
it would devastate her if the boy did not
recover.

For the next two days they fell into an odd
routine. Emily continued to do all she could
for Thornton, and Cloud periodically
dragged her from the child's side for an
enforced rest. While he never offered her
false hopes, he gave her sympathy and tried
to soothe her growing fears. The longer the
boy remained ill, however, the harder Cloud
found it to comfort her. He could not help

doubting that such a small boy could fight off such a virulent fever for much longer.

Emily felt as if she had not slept in days. James and Cloud were sprawled on the floor, sound asleep but determined to be close at hand if she needed them. She wished she could join them but feared giving in to her exhaustion too completely. So too was she increasingly afraid to leave Thornton's side, afraid that, if she did, he would slip away from her.

Sitting by the bed, she rested her head on her arms, one hand lightly touching Thornton's. Despite her efforts to stay awake, her eyes closed. She told herself she would only take a brief rest before bathing him again.

With a groan, Emily swatted at the hand patting her on the head. Then her eyes flew open when a testy little voice said, "Whatcha sleeping there for? Wake up, Mama. I'm kinda hungry."

She sat up straight and stared at the little boy looking at her with bright eyes clear of all sign of fever. The light in the cabin told her she had slept through the night. Pressing one hand to her trembling lips, she reached out an unsteady hand to feel the boy's forehead and cheeks.

"Oh, thank the sweet Lord, you're cool. So beautifuly cool."

"I'm kinda wet too, Mama."

"Cloud!"

Cloud bolted to his feet. His heart clenched briefly in fear, sure that Emily's screech was because the boy had died in the night. Then he saw Thornton sitting up looking startled as Emily hugged him and peppered his small face with kisses. He nudged James awake and the two of them soon joined in the celebration of the boy's recovery until Thornton rather loudly demanded some food.

Looking at Cloud, who held her in his arms, Emily noticed a suspicious sheen to his eyes. "Why, Cloud, you . . ."

Setting her on her feet, he pulled a stern face, patted her on the backside, and ordered, "Shut up, woman, and get the boy some food."

Laughing softly she hurried to do so, deciding she would be nice and not tell Cloud what a fraud he was.

Chapter Ten

"This is a town?"

Emily tried to be understanding and not to use her more settled and older place of birth as a comparison. She failed. No amount of understanding or tolerance could turn the collection of tents, ramshackle huts, and mud spread out before her into a town. She was not sure it would be good for the health of any of them to enter such a place and prayed that Lockridge would be better.

"Yup. It's called Promise," Cloud replied, unable to fully repress a smile over the look on Emily's face.

"It does not appear to have much."

"Nope, it doesn't and it'll soon disappear into the mud. I'm surprised it's still here."

"Exactly why is it here?" She nudged Carolynn to follow Cloud as he started off again.

"Gold, honey. Someone found a trace. Trouble is, it was a weak vein not producing much, although there must still be enough trickling in to keep folk here and hoping. We're headed to the house at the other end of town." He smothered a laugh when James sent him a totally shocked look behind Emily's back.

Looking up ahead, Emily's eyes widened slightly in surprise. At the far end of town was a large, sturdy two-story building. It was nothing special, except that it looked clean, actually having grass around it. Emily thought it looked like an oasis within the squalor that surrounded it. She just hoped that it was not going to prove the residence of yet another of Cloud's women.

They had barely finished dismounting when a plump woman bustled out of the house and gave Cloud a hearty hug. Emily was a little surprised by the matronly woman's attire, which was quite gaudy, but she silently allowed Cloud to tow her after him as he followed the chattering woman into the house. She wondered why James seemed reluctant to enter the house and kept sending her decidedly worried glances.

"Brought your own this time, have you, boy? I won't make much money if everyone starts to do that."

"This is Emily. Emily, meet Mrs. Little. Eliza Little."

Holding out her hand, Emily smiled gently. "Pleased to meet you, Mrs. Little. You are most kind to grant us your hospitality." She frowned when the woman shook her hand somewhat limply and came very close to gaping widely.

"Ke-rist, Cloud, you done brought a lady in here! What're you thinking of? You trying to ruin me? I thought we was friends."

Cloud put his arm around the woman's shoulders and urged her away from Emily. "Now, Liza, Em won't do you any harm."

"She's a lady. Some eastern highborn by the sounds coming outta her. She can't do me any good, that's for plain and certain."

"Emily will do nothing to hurt you. I swear it, Liza. We need a place for the night, and this is the cleanest and the safest." Seeing that the woman needed some more persuading, Cloud told her some of Emily's troubles, soon winning the woman's sympathy.

As Cloud had a murmured exchange with Mrs. Little, Emily finally took a good look around. Her first impression was that the place was far plusher inside than the outside indicated. Then she looked a little closer and began to feel very uneasy.

Stepping closer to a painting on the wall, she turned her eyes away after one look. She was certain there was only one sort of place that would have a painting portraying such intimate activities. A brief, horrified look at a piece of statuary nearby confirmed her growing suspicions. She looked at a grimacing James in shock.

"She's guessed, Cloud."

Turning at James's call and looking at Emily, Cloud choked on a laugh. He had never seen her blush so deeply. A laugh was even harder to suppress when one of Liza's girls, the beauteous Jasmine, strolled into the room wearing only enough to cover what was strictly necessary, and Emily immediately covered Thornton's eyes.

"Cloud," Emily whispered, trying very hard not to stare at the nearly naked woman. "Might I have a word with you?"

"Didn't you tell her where you were bringing her?" Eliza asked Cloud.

"Nope. Looks like I'm going to hear about it now though, Liza."

"I wouldn't sound so cheerful about it, lad. She looks like one mad little lady. You sure she won't cause me any trouble?"

"Very sure. Well, so long as I get her out of sight before your customers start to wander in."

"Ain't that the truth."

"Cloud." Emily tried hard not to snap but could not fully repress the hint of her rising temper in her voice.

"Now, Em," he said as he stepped over to her.

"I am beginning to consider those two

words very ominous. However, this time I believe I would greatly appreciate it if you are about to tell me that I am simply foolish and that you have not brought me and Thornton to a—a house of—of ill-repute."

"Here now, I got a good reputation," Liza sputtered. "I'm an honest woman."

"I was not impunging your honesty, Mrs. Little. The expression refers to—er, what goes on here." She looked at Cloud, waiting for an answer.

"Well, I'm afraid you have it right this time, darlin'. This is a bawdy house."

Since a large part of her had hoped he would deny it, Emily was even more shocked. "Cloud, how could you—?"

Gently grasping her by the shoulders he smiled faintly as he looked into her wide eyes. "I did it because this place is clean and safe. Thornton needs a good, clean place to sleep in, especially after he was ill not so long ago. So do you. The other place in town is a rat-infested cesspit. No place in this town would be safe for you. I figure you're fair sick of fighting and shooting, but you'd get a hell of a lot of both if we stayed anywhere in Promise but here. You can't tell me you didn't see how they all looked at you as we rode here."

Recalling all the gazes that had been fixed upon her and how nervous they had made her, Emily made no attempt to deny that. "But, Cloud, what about Thornton? Surely it is not good for him . . ."

Reaching down to remove her hands from the boy's eyes, he said quietly, "Thornton is too young to know he's seeing anything he shouldn't and he'll be tucked up and sleeping before the—er, business here really gets started. Liza's always got a couple of rooms left empty we can use."

"That's right, miss," Liza chimed in. "I'll show you and the boy to one now, if you'd like." She winked at Cloud. "I reckon Cloud and James will be a while making their choices."

"As you said, Liza, I brought my own." He ignored Emily's groan. "Em and me'll share a room. James and Thornton'll take another."

"You and her? But, I—I mean, she's a lady."

"Unfortunately, Mrs. Little," Emily said, after glaring briefly at Cloud, who never failed to reveal his total lack of discretion, "this lady had the misfortune to stumble upon a rogue."

Liza chuckled. "He's that, all right. The girls'll be sore disappointed."

"That seems to be the lot of half of the females in the Colorado Territory," Emily muttered and decided that Cloud was ill-mannered to grin like that.

Liza laughed heartily over Emily's remark, but James still looked worried.

"Um, Cloud? If you'll excuse us a moment,

ladies. Cloud, I'd like to have a word with you," James said quietly.

"Well?"

"It might be better said private-like."

"Spit it out, James."

A light color touched James's cheekbones but he doggedly proceeded. "Look, Cloud, I have been traveling with you a long time."

"Since Justine."

Grinning at Emily, James continued, "It's been real nice, but while you've had Em to hold—Sorry, Em. Anyways, I've been with the boy. I'm real fond of Thornton, but now we're here I think tonight I'd like a—well . . ."

"Of course you would," Liza said when James faltered. "Little Thornton can bed with me." She smiled when Emily could not fully repress a frown of concern. "I just run the business. I ain't got any interest in the rest. Now, let me show you to the rooms I got. You can have a bath if you want, then we can have supper."

"Who'd you lose, Liza?" Cloud asked as, after collecting the bags, they followed the woman upstairs.

"Lucy and Tiffany."

"Tiffany? Don't think I know that one."

"What a surprise," Emily murmured.

Liza chuckled and answered, "She wasn't here long. Got left behind by a gambling man so she came here to work, then took off with another gambling man. Fool girl. Now, Lucy up and wed one of the miners."

Emily only half listened to the conversation. She did not really wish to hear how well acquainted Cloud was with all of Liza's "workers." Her air of disinterest vanished, however, when she and Cloud were shown to a room, promised a bath and left alone.

Wide-eyed with shock, she stared at the room. The bed was large and canopied, its covers red and gold. There were mirrors everywhere. After spotting several rather lewd paintings she turned to stare at Cloud, who watched her warily.

"Em, it really is the best place to stay tonight. Safest and cleanest, I swear it."

"But it is so—so vulgar."

"Yeh, to you, I reckon it is. I never really noticed."

Busying herself with removing her hat, Emily sighed. "I am not sure I wish to spend a night in a place filled with women you have—er, known well. Meeting them one at a time was tedious enough."

Hiding a smile, Cloud moved to stand behind her. Putting his arms around her, he kissed the nape of her neck. Such remarks gave him the hint that Emily's feelings ran deeper than desire alone. That, he knew, could only benefit him. He discovered that he was ridiculously pleased by each such hint.

"Em, whatever I did here in the past was bought and paid for. Hardly something worth bothering about. A business transaction."

That was faintly comforting. By the time they joined Liza, James, and Thornton for supper, she was not sure it was true, however, at least not on the part of the women. Each one they met as they made their way to the kitchen had boldly invited Cloud to her bed, made a reference or two to past encounters, and made it clear that the value of his coin was not what prompted their interest. Thoroughly disgusted and achingly jealous, Emily gave Liza all her attention and found the woman interesting as well as humorous. She was sorry to be parted from her when they were surreptitiously returned to their room as the customers began to arrive.

Although it troubled her deeply when Cloud left her alone to go and play cards with Liza, she hid it. If he were intending to answer some of the invitations hurled his way, there was little she could do about it. As she crawled into bed, she wished she could accept that instead of having doubts and fears gnaw at her, keeping her awake. She put the pillow over her head to block out the increasing noise and wished she could as easily block out the images jealousy put in her mind.

"It's getting late, son," Liza said as she idly shuffled the cards.

"One more hand. I still have the vain hope

I'll do more than break even with you, Liza."

She laughed and dealt the cards. "She's a cute little thing, your Em. Real polite too. That's good breeding, that is."

He nodded. "She's got that all right." He frowned slightly. "It seems a little rowdier here than it used to be."

"That's desperation you hear. They know this town is dying, that they'll have to move on. Men can get a little wild when they know all their dreams're worth squat. Haven't had any real trouble, though. Your Em'll be safe."

Even as Liza spoke, a scream pierced through all the other sounds in the house. Cursing viciously, Cloud bolted toward the stairs. Liza hurried after him but was hard put just to keep him in view.

Using curses she had learned from Cloud, Emily fought to get out from beneath the big, hairy, and very drunk man who had sprawled on top of her, waking her out of a sound sleep. He kept calling her Tiffany, but he was too drunk to heed her denials. In the increasingly vain hope that someone would hear her and come to help her, she screamed and screamed again. She was just about to do so a third time when the door to the room was slammed open and, an instant later, her attacker was ripped off of her. Emily saw Cloud fling the larger man to the floor, then saw a panting Liza appear in the doorway.

To Emily's extreme embarrassment, a half-dozen people quickly appeared behind Liza to peer in at her. Emily yanked the sheet up to her neck.

"Easy now, Cloud," Liza said. "That's Jake and he's harmless enough. He's drunk, too. Thinks your lady's Tiffany, I'll wager."

"Yes, he did keep calling me that."

After a searching look over Emily, which revealed her frightened but apparently unhurt, Cloud looked at Liza. "How the hell'd he get in here? The door was locked."

"Reckon Tiffany gave him a key. Girl never did follow rules. Joe, Leroy, get this fool friend of yours outta here and try to make him understand Tiffany ain't here no more." Even as the two men hurried to pick up a dazed Jake, Liza fished through his pockets and got the key. "Damnation. Hope that fool girl didn't hand out any others. You all right, miss?"

"Just frightened, Mrs. Little. I was asleep and suddenly he was there."

"That'd startle a body all right. Reckon that ends our card game, Cloud. See you at breakfast."

"Yeh, thanks, Liza." As soon as he had shut the door after everyone and locked it, Cloud looked at Emily. "You sure you're all right?"

"I thought you said this place was safe." She hopped out of bed, hurried over to the washbowl and proceeded to scrub her mouth clean, needing to be rid of the whiskey-soured taste of her inept attacker. "I swear I have not been safe since I left Boston. I have been leered at, propositioned, compromised, kidnapped, held at knife point and attacked by a drunken sot wailing for a Tiffany."

She glared at Cloud as she stomped back to the bed and got in with a decided flounce. "Now I find myself sleeping in a room where every place I look I find myself staring back at me. It would serve this territory right if I wrote a letter to all the papers back east enumerating every travail I have endured."

He could not fully suppress the laughter in his voice as he exclaimed, "Hell, Em, if you did that, no woman'd travel west of the Mississippi." He started to undress.

"Exactly. Not many men would either, for their wives would sit down in St. Louis or Independence and refuse to take another step."

Shaking his head and laughing softly, he shed the last of his clothes and slid into bed beside her. "You're in a real snit, aren't you?"

Although still tense with anger, she did not resist when he tugged her into his arms. "I was sleeping peacefully and was rudely awakened by a huge, hairy man stinking of whiskey and a great deal more. It was not a pleasant experience."

"Poor Em. I'm sorry. It is safe here. Trust

me. You would've been perfectly safe if that girl, Tiffany, had stuck to the rules. Liza doesn't allow room keys handed out. If nothing else, it would allow for some private—er, interaction, which is like stealing from her. It's also dangerous. It means someone can get in and out of a room with one of her girls without her knowing who, when or where. She'd lose control over the situation and that could lead to some real trouble."

He slowly stroked and nuzzled away her anger and the touch of fear that lingered. Once he was certain that she was fully responding, he made slow, gentle love to her. Ruthlessly ignoring her protests and changing them to cries of delight, he left no part of her untouched or untasted. She turned to fire in his arms and he revealed it.

Emily peeked at the man sprawled in her arms, blushed, and looked away. She could not believe the things she had allowed him to do nor the way she had responded to his intimate kisses. Although she could not believe Cloud was given to any strange perversions, she could not fully believe that the intimacies they had just shared were quite right.

Glancing up at Emily, Cloud smiled faintly over the color staining her cheeks. He was not surprised to find her fretting over her abandonment in his arms once the glow of passion had faded. Her innocence and modesty insured her embarrassment. He simply hoped he could think of all the right words to soothe her, for tasting Emily from her now furrowed brow to her delicate little toes, with a lot of lingering in between, was something he decided he had a positive craving for. Pleasuring Emily in such a way was a pleasure for him and not simply a rarely used and calculated move to ready her for him to seek his own gratification.

"Em, you think too much." He nuzzled her neck. "Sometimes it's best just to feel, just to enjoy."

She sighed and wished it could be so easy. "I do not know if I can. Some things seem so scandalous they cannot possibly be right."

"Trust me, Em. I'm not given to any strange twists of taste."

"Well, I couldn't really believe that you were."

"I'm not. If it's something that pleasures us both, I figure it's okay. You're a prude, Em," he goaded.

"Quite probably, although I hardly think that my finding it shocking to roll about in total abandonment with a man who is not my lawful husband is prudish. That should shock anyone with a sense of modesty or morality."

Rolling onto his back, he dragged her on top of him and winked at her. "Total abandonment, hmmm? I like the sound of that."

"Yes, you would." A sound much like an Indian's war whoop echoed through the hall and Emily gasped. "Cloud? Did you hear that?" Her first start of fear faded rapidly when she realized that Cloud was laughing. "Stop laughing and tell me what it was." When he just laughed harder, she suddenly realized what had caused the sound and blushed even as it echoed through the hall again. "Oh."

"Old James sure must be enjoying himself."

At first Emily was embarrassed, but then curiosity proved stronger. "That was James? No, it can't be. He is such a gentleman."

"Oh, it's James all right. Honey, you put a man in a bed with a willing woman and his fine manners slip away fast."

"Well, I wouldn't know about that, seeing as the only man I have been in a bed with doesn't have any fine manners to let slip," she drawled, then ruined the effects of her coolly delivered insult by giggling over his mock look of outrage.

For a little while they playfully wrestled, and Cloud discovered that Emily was ticklish nearly everywhere and Emily discovered that Cloud had only one ticklish spot—the bottom of his feet—but that it was a very ticklish spot indeed. When they finally stopped their nonsense, Cloud was sprawled on top of her and they were both breathing heavily. A moment later Emily realized that it was not only Cloud's laughter that had been stirred by their tussling.

"Again?"

"Got some objections, do you?"

Since his skillful stroking was already making her purr softly, Emily decided that that was a very foolish question.

Unsuccessfully smothering a yawn, Cloud adjusted an equally sleepy Emily more comfortably in his arms. "Your journey will be over soon, darlin'. A week left at the most."

Emily felt as if someone had just punched her in the heart. She had realized that they were getting close to the San Luis Valley, but she had not realized that they were quite that close. Reluctantly, she admitted to herself that she had not thought about it, had indeed done her best not to think about it. She felt panicked about how little time there was left. It seemed far too short a time to make any further headway into Cloud's heart. She could not help but feel that she had lost the battle for his love.

"Only a week?" She hoped he would attribute the soft huskiness of her voice to weariness and not guess that she was very close to bursting into tears.

"Or less. The last leg of our journey could go smoothly, but I never bet on it. Soon you'll see that brother of yours."

"That will be nice." And you will drop me at his doorstep like a lump of hot coals, she thought despairingly.

Chapter Eleven

Dawn was just streaking the sky when Cloud nudged Emily awake. He felt a sense of rising excitement. Wolfe's ranch was not quite a day's ride away. Not only would he see his brother for the first time in almost a year, but he would be back on his own land. He realized that it was the first time since he had bought the plot of land that he was eager to see it, to get planning on what to do with it. Glancing at the delicate woman who was sitting up and rubbing her eyes, he had the feeling she had something to do with his change of attitude. She had started him planning, was part of his thoughts on the future.

"Cheer up, Emily. This is the last day you

have to ride Carolynn."

She managed a smile, then watched as he moved to check on the coffee he was already brewing. He was obviously in high spirits and that hurt. It might not be because he would soon be rid of her, but there was no ignoring the fact that that was what would happen soon. She would be dutifully delivered to her brother by the day's end.

Trying to shake off her sadness, she tended to Thornton. Soon she was caught up in the many chores entailed in breaking camp. The work kept her from brooding, but she could not fully shake her depression. When she was finally mounted and riding there was so little to distract her that she felt almost overwhelmed by sadness. It took most of her concentration simply to keep herself from weeping.

Cloud kept glancing at Emily but her crestfallen expression did not change. He had seen her in all sorts of moods but never so sad, and he decided he did not like it.

When they stopped at noon for a brief rest and a light meal, Cloud managed to manuever Emily to a spot that gave them a little privacy. As he watched her pick at the bread and cheese Mrs. Little had kindly given them, he wondered what to say or do to pull her out of her mood.

"Em, is anything wrong?"

Barely glancing at him, she shook her head. "No, nothing. I am just weary."

"Well, you'll have a proper bed to sleep in tonight."

"That will be nice." She managed a smile. "And a bath?"

"A hot one."

"That will be heaven."

After a few more vain attempts at conversation. Cloud gave up and joined James, who watched Thornton as the boy crouched in some long grass searching for interesting bugs. He sat down by his friend, and said, "Something's bothering Emily."

"Just noticed that, did you?"

"No," he snapped. "I noticed it from the start. What I want to know is what the hell is it?"

"Is the great womanizer of the West asking advice from a novice like me?" James met Cloud's furious look with a smile. "Why don't you just ask her what's bothering her? Simple's sometimes the best."

"I did ask her. If she didn't consider it indelicate, she would probably just grunt. Being such a polite little thing, she does give me at least two, three words at a time. She's telling me diddly. I'm up against a wall. Hell, she looks ready to cry."

"And that'd bother you, would it?"

"Yeh," Cloud ground out. "How about a little help here?"

"Well, the only thought I have is probably not one you want to hear." He glanced toward Thornton to assure himself that the boy was not wandering away.

"I'll listen to anything at the moment." Cloud ran a hand through his hair in an uncharacteristic gesture of frustration. "Think it's her female time? Women can get strange then."

"Nope, what I think ails her is that, very soon, you'll be dropping her at her brother's doorstep like so much excess baggage."

"And who said I was going to do that?"

"It was the plan, wasn't it?"

"It was." Cloud did not feel like telling anyone what he had decided just yet. "Maybe I've changed my mind."

"Going to keep her?"

"Well, I ain't dropping her at Harper's door like—what did you say?—so much excess baggage."

"Did you tell her that?"

"Nope."

"Then perhaps you should."

"Thought I'd wait until we could be private at Wolfe's."

"Then get used to her mood, for I suspect it'll be around until you do."

"You really think that's the problem?"

"Seems the most logical. Girl does have some pride if nothing else."

Cloud nodded absently. James's theory cheered him. If that was what made Emily look so forlorn, it meant she had some feeling for him and would like to stay with him. His proposal would probably have a good chance of being accepted.

For a moment he was tempted to propose immediately, but he resisted that urge. He wanted to be able to at least tell her what sort of life he planned on, and he was not quite ready to do that. It would take a week or two before he had any set ideas or plans to set before her. Then he would propose. He was sure she would be safe at Harper's until he did. He kept that decision firm while stoutly refusing to think on how he would be sleeping alone during that time.

It was late in the afternoon when Cloud rode up beside her and pointed to a large ranch house in the distance. "That's Wolfe's place. He's worked on it some since I last saw it." Cloud halted for a moment.

Emily was pleasantly surprised by what she saw. After the places they had stopped at on the way, she had expected something much rougher. It was no Boston mansion, but it was a far cry from a two-room cabin.

"It's very nice."

"Our pa was a farmer, but he had a real skill at building too. He taught us everything he knew."

"Wolfe lives there alone?"

"For now. He decided he might as well build big because he plans to stay and had the funds to do it."

"Very sensible."

"Well, let's go fill up his house."

That remark puzzled her, but before she could ask exactly what he meant, Cloud was starting toward the house. She nudged her horse to follow him and hoped that he would recall his promise of a hot bath. Glancing at the sky, which aleady held the promise of night, she hoped she would have the time before he hurried her off to Harper's.

Even as they reined in before the house, a tall young man stepped out. Cloud vaulted from the saddle and the two were soon laughing and roughly embracing each other. She noticed that there was a strong family resemblance between the pair as James helped first Thornton, then her down from their horses. It was impossible not to wonder if Wolfe Ryder was as great a libertine as his brother. When men looked like that, she mused a little bitterly, it was probably inevitable.

Wolfe Ryder's eyes were the color of amber. She murmured a response to his friendly greeting and wondered, a little wildly, if anyone in the Ryder family had eyes of a common color.

Things grew very confusing for a while. Wolfe mistakenly tried to put her in with James, only to be sharply corrected by Cloud. She got no chance to ask about when she would be taken to Harper's and soon found herself alone in the room she had been shown to, a steaming bath readied and waiting for her. Setting aside all her questions a little while longer, she started to shed her dusty clothes.

Sinking into the hot water with a sigh of near ecstasy, Emily felt almost cheerful.

There was nothing, she decided, that could better soothe any pain than a soak in a hot bath. She hoped it would work to lift her spirits. There was very little time left to be with Cloud and she did not want to spend it sulking. Closing her eyes as she soaked, she told herself firmly that she would not give Cloud any reason to think that his callous disposal of her mattered one little bit.

Cloud frowned as he watched Emily seated across from him at the kitchen table. She was in much better spirits and, although the meal Wolfe had set before them was hearty, he doubted it was the cause of her greatly improved mood. It irritated him, for he could no longer feel certain that she cared about leaving him.

"By the way, Cloud," she asked, interrupting his increasingly dark thoughts. "When do I go to Harper's?"

"In the morning."

It was not only his curt reply that surprised her but the news that she still had one more night with him. She was cross that he was so slow to tell her what plans had been made, but she quickly shook that irritation aside. She was being given one more night with Cloud and she was determined to make the best of it. It could well be the last chance she had to change his mind about leaving her and to make a few more memories to cherish in what began to look like a very barren future.

No one, she thought, would ever be able to take away her memories and she decided she would do her best to make some heady ones. It was a scandalous plan, but her whole time with Cloud had been scandalous. She had been very good up until she had met him and would undoubtedly be painfully good after he left her. A little scandal would not kill her, she told herself firmly to silence that part of her that seemed continually shocked since she had met Cloud.

By the time they retired for the night, Cloud had gone far past irritation. He told himself it was because he had made plans and did not like having to change them, but he did not really believe it. For the first time in his life, he did not want to be rid of a woman, but Emily was beginning to show every sign of being glad to be rid of him. What added to his anger was that it hurt him, something no woman had done since he was very young and very naive.

Sitting on the edge of the bed to remove his boots, he covertly watched her as she readied herself for bed. She was, he mused, one of the most innately graceful women he had ever seen. He doubted it was all due to good breeding and the lessons of society. With Emily, he suspected it was mostly natural, done without thought.

The thought of her background made him scowl. He had never really considered the fact that it could be a problem and that might have been extraordinarily blind of him. She was a lady, Boston bred and educated. He was part Indian, mostly self-taught, and a poor farmer's son. A match between them was something that most people, possibly even including his own family, would think impossible if not laughable, despite the fact that he had bedded her.

Seeing Cloud's scowl in the mirror as she finished brushing her hair, Emily sighed. It was going to be very hard to make any sweet memories when the man she wished to make them with was acting as grouchy as a bear with a sore paw. That was not the only reason she started to get annoyed, however. She could think of nothing she had done to deserve the glares he directed at her. Putting down the brush with a distinct snap, she went to the bed and climbed in with what even she saw as a flounce.

"If you have no wish to share this room with me, why not just say so instead of staying on and acting so put out?"

As he stood up to shed his pants Cloud stared at her in slight surprise. He had been momentarily distracted from his growing anger by watching her lithe body, barely kept modest by the shift she wore, as she had flounced to the bed. It took him a moment to realize why she should say such a thing. She was clearly putting her own interpretation on his evident annoyance.

"If I didn't want to share this room and this bed with you I wouldn't have even walked in that door." He joined her in bed and caught her hand when she reached out to turn down the lamp.

"Then have I offended your brother? Committed some grave faux pas? There must be some reason for the way you have been glaring at me since dinner."

Tugging her into his arms he slid his hands up the back of her legs to cup her shapely backside. "You weren't getting to bed fast enough."

He watched her carefully as he brushed light kisses over her face. As always her eyes began to grow heavy-lidded, the green darkening with the hint of her growing passion. It told him that, although she might be thinking herself glad to be rid of him, she had not been able to dim her desire for him. She might think it was over, he mused as he tugged off her shift, but it was not.

Emily met his gaze as he pressed her flesh against his. Passion was darkening the depths of his eyes, but anger still lingered. She pushed against him, trying to free herself, but his hold on her simply tightened.

"You are still angry with me. I don't want"—she hesitated but was unable to find any words—"this done in anger."

"You're damned glad to be seeing Harper tomorrow, aren't you?"

She blinked, feeling confused, a state of mind greatly contributed to by the way he was stroking her in all the right places. "Well, yes. Of course. I haven't seen my brother in far too long."

Pushing her onto her back, he crouched over her. "Maybe it ain't anger you see, but determination."

"Determination?" The word came out as a gasp for he began to lathe the tips of her breasts with his tongue.

For a moment she forgot what they were talking about. She burrowed her fingers into his hair, holding his head against her breasts. The way he gently kneaded their fullness with his hands, skillfully teased the tips with his tongue until they ached, and then soothed that torment by drawing the hardened nub deep into his mouth, made her desire soar and thought nearly impossible.

"A determination to be sure that you don't get to pleased to see Harper that you forget the last weeks and just who you spent them with." He brushed soft kisses over her midriff and felt her buck slightly when he teased at her navel with his tongue.

Cloud intended to mark her as his. He wanted to brand her in flesh and mind so firmly that her skin would still heat with the memory of him for weeks to come. For a while he would not be able to keep a close watch on her, so he would leave her with a memory so strong it would prove guard enough.

As he stroked her thighs with his lips and hands, Emily found it impossible to speak clearly. She had the feeling he meant for her to be so enthralled. When his lips brushed the very top of her thigh she knew what he planned to do to her. Still uncertain about that intimacy, she tried to pull away but he held her still with ease. She cried out when the warmth of his mouth touched the very center point of her desire. In another instant she no longer cared about what he had been saying or what his mood was; she simply wanted him, craved the pleasure he was giving her.

When he finally responded to her cries and plunged into her, she clung to him tightly. Although her release was quick and fierce, he was soon joining her in the fall into desire's abyss. It was not until her senses began to return to normal that she began to suspect that his lovemaking had been inspired by more than a need to give and get pleasure. She began to feel a little as if she had been used. It left her confused and hurt, for she was not sure why he had acted so, whether or not his reasons would simply hurt her more. It was that thought that kept her silent until his actions told her that he intended to make love to her again.

Pushing him away, she said quietly, "I think I have had enough of your games." She turned onto her side.

Staring at her stiff, slim back, Cloud felt a twinge of guilt. He also found it uncomfortable to be read with such apparent ease. Slipping an arm around her waist, he kissed her shoulder and ignored her tenseness. The last thing he wanted was to push her away with his actions.

"Em, I wasn't playing games."

"Why don't I believe that?"

"I was deadly serious," he said quietly and met her gaze squarely when she turned to look at him.

"Determined?" She suddenly recalled the somewhat confusing things he had said earlier, things that she still did not understand even with a clear head.

"Right, determined. I'm going to be leaving you with Harper for a while."

"Of course. That has always been the plan." She frowned. "What do you mean— for a while?"

"Well, for a while without seeing you." He was still reluctant to talk of the future he had planned and knew he would have to be careful in what he said. "Or would you rather I didn't come to see you?"

"Oh, no. I should like to see you." She had to bite her tongue to keep from telling him exactly how much.

"Then why the hell have you been so damned cheerful all evening?"

Her eyes widened and she nearly laughed. All her efforts at making him believe she was not bothered by their impending separation had clearly worked, but not in exactly the manner she had intended. Then she frowned. If he had had something in mind other than leaving her at Harper's doorstep and walking away, he should have mentioned it sometime during all the weeks they had been together. If nothing else, it would have been a kindness on his part. Instead, it seemed he had kept all his thoughts to himself, then gotten annoyed when she did not fall in with the plans he had made.

"I graciously decided that I would not burden you with any troubles, emotional or otherwise. I did not wish to be some irksome female who did not know when her time with you had come to an end. I did not wish to end up treated as you have treated Janice and—" The list she had been about to recite was ended by a quick, hard kiss.

"You'd never be treated like that."

"I have had no reason to think otherwise." She thought briefly that that might not be quite true, but then decided that it would not hurt him to argue it and might even result in an easing of the hurt he could so easily, and unthinkingly, inflict.

He frowned at her. It did not seem to him that he had treated her as he had other women. In fact, he was sure he had not. Every aspect of their relationship had been different from any other he had had before her. Somehow he had not made her see that, but he was not sure how to rectify his mistake. Neither did he want to say things to soothe her that he was not ready to say yet or did not feel. The flat truth, except for his thoughts about marriage, would have to do.

"If I've left you thinking you're no more to me than a Justine or the others, I'm sorry. I didn't think I had."

"Well, perhaps not," she mumbled, honesty forcing her to admit to it. "Then again, you've never once led me to believe that you planned anything other than just what we had agreed upon at the start—you would take me to Harper's."

"There's a good reason for that. I had to be sure I wanted to do something else. I sure as hell wasn't going to tell you until I was sure. Since I've never wanted to keep on seeing a woman so much for so long before, I doubted I knew what I wanted." He grimaced and ran a hand through his hair. "I'm not explaining this very well, am I."

"You're not doing too badly." She smiled faintly, beginning to understand his silence on the matter even if she did wish he had not been so reticent. "To speak of it could be seen as a promise and one you could later decide you did not want to keep."

Cloud nodded and realized that that was one of things he really appreciated about her. She seemed to try very hard not to let emotion rule her thoughts or common sense. Also, while she might not agree with one's reasoning, she did listen carefully to it and try to understand. As a result he found it easy to talk to her and he was more open with her than he had ever been with a woman. That, he knew, could only benefit them in the future.

"Exactly. I've always been wary of making any sort of promise."

The thought that there could yet be a

chance of a future for them cheered Emily immensely. Although she warned herself about letting her hopes rise, she could not fully stop herself from hoping. He was not going to simply discard her as he had so many in the past—at least not immediately. There was no ignoring the fact that that gave her a chance. She would have time, the time she craved to continue to try and win some place in his heart.

"So, I was being tested, was I?" She draped her arms around his neck and pressed closer to him.

Putting his arms around her and pressing her even closer, he murmured a little guiltily, "Reckon you were."

"And I passed?" She slowly slid one hand down his back to stroke his hip and felt his increasing arousal.

"With flying colors." Since she seemed calmly accepting, he saw no reason to be evasive and, as her hand moved from his hip to his groin, he decided he was no longer interested in the conversation anyway.

Watching his eyes grow heavy-lidded, Emily smiled faintly as she felt her own desire stirred by the evidence of how she could arouse him. "So, are you going to court me, then?"

"Hmmm? Oh, right. Yeh."

"Bring me flowers and sweets?"

"Sure. Whatever." He frowned as he cleared his passion-fogged mind enough to think about what he was agreeing to. "Wrong time of the year for flowers. Wasn't thinking on being too fancy."

That did not surprise her at all. Cloud was not a man to indulge in such trappings. She knew she would not miss any of it, but could not resist teasing him.

"And serenade me below my window."

Realizing he was being teased even before she started to grin, he growled softly and, turning onto his back, pulled her on top of him. "Listen real close, Em, and I'll serenade you."

She laughed softly but soon had to agree that it was very much like beautiful music.

Chapter Twelve

"You can probably meet the rest of the clan in the spring."

"That would be nice."

Cloud almost smiled at her absently given response. He glanced at her where she sat next to him on the wagon, then reined the team to a halt. Before she could say a word, he tugged her into his arms and heartily kissed her.

"Blech!" came a protesting voice behind them.

Laughing softly, Cloud released Emily and turned to ruffle Thornton's curly hair. "Enough out of you." Picking up the reins, he started them on their way again.

Finally catching her breath, Emily asked

dazedly, "What was that for?"

"You seemed to be distracted." He leaned over and asked softly, "Sure you don't want Thornton to stay with me?"

"Let us see how Harper and Dorothy act. It may be vanity, but I think, even though he does like you a lot, he might be more content to stay with me." She frowned. "Unless you think . . ."

"I think it's not vanity. He would be more content with you. Kid his age needs a mother and he sees you as that."

She smiled crookedly. "I know, and sometimes it can feel a little odd. Having motherhood thrust upon one can be confusing at best." Glancing back at Thornton, she saw the boy leaning out over the back of the wagon. "Careful, Thornton. You might fall out. Please stay to the middle. That's a good boy," she said gently when he obeyed.

"You sure sound like a mother," Cloud drawled and grinned when she eyed him suspiciously. "No insult meant. I swear it."

After another moment of riding silently, Emily found her thoughts drifting again. She was feeling increasingly nervous about meeting her brother again after so many years. His wife was a complete stranger to her. In fact, Harper had said very little about his wife, Dorothy. Emily was not sure that was a very good sign.

"Emily."

Hearing the faint note of irritation in

Cloud's voice, she grimaced. "Was I ignoring you again?"

"Not really. I wasn't saying anything. Look, Em, if you don't feel right about going, we'll turn around now, go back to Wolfe's."

"Well, to be perfectly honest, I feel very unsure about this, but I'll still go. That was the whole point of this journey, of why I left Boston. Also, Harper is expecting me. Why, he might even have heard about the tragedy and think I'm dead."

"I feel sure we're here before the ill-fated group would have got this far. I doubt he's heard the news, Em. News travels slow out here." There was a chance that one of the places they had stopped at and where he had reported the massacre could have sent word out, but he decided it was not worth worrying her about. "All I want to know is if you're sure about this. You've got a choice."

"Not really. Even if I didn't go now, he is sure to find out that I'm in the area. Then he'll wonder why I haven't come to him. No." She shook her head. "I'm just being foolishly nervous. It's just because it has been so long since I last saw him."

Cloud just nodded, keeping his thoughts to himself. He had met Dorothy Brockinger a few times. She was a cold, tight-lipped woman despite the looks of welcome she sent him. It was something he had not thought about until he set Emily in the wagon and started towards Harper's. Emily was not going to find living with Dorothy easy. Cloud felt sure that Dorothy Brockinger was one of those women who would avidly resent a younger, prettier female sharing her home. Sharing such knowledge with Emily would do her no good and he did not have to leave her at Harper's for long anyway.

Glancing her way, he caught her trying to hide a yawn behind her hand and drawled, "Tired?"

Despite her efforts not to, Emily felt herself blush. After the way she and Cloud had carried on all through the night and even before they had risen in the morning, blushes were completely justified. She managed, however, to give him a creditable look of haughty boredom.

"Not at all."

He laughed softly. " 'Course not. Here, we'll be in town, more or less, in a minute. Last chance to change your mind."

She shook her head, even though her hands were clenched together in her lap. There was something she had to speak to Cloud about, and it was now or never. She took a deep breath to steady her nerves.

"Cloud?"

"Changed your mind?"

"No. You won't—well, let Harper know everything about our journey here, will you?" She stared at her hands. "I really could not bear the trouble it might cause."

"Em, all that's strictly between us. Ain't his business."

"Thank you."

"It hasn't exactly been a secret though."

"I know." She shrugged. "But there's no need to walk in the door, set down my bag, and slap him in the face with the news."

" 'Course not. He won't hear it from me."

It was hard not to tell her that he planned to do right by her. Just as he had feared, she seemed to be worrying about shame and sin and all that again. It was another reason to get her out of Harper's house as soon as he could. He did not want her to think that way for too long. He promised himself that he would set his plans straight as soon as he could.

The house Cloud stopped before surprised Emily a little. Harper had said that he was doing well, but she had not thought he would appear so above his neighbors. The house looked somewhat out of place, a little too much like wealthy New England.

After lifting Thornton from the wagon, Cloud helped Emily down. He watched her covertly as he took her bags from the wagon. She looked painfully nervous. That did little to help end the wavering of his resolve to leave her with her brother. He had to remind himself that it was really for the best. If nothing else, by taking her to Harper's so quickly after arriving, it would still some of the rumors that were bound to circulate once people knew he had been the one to bring her in. He could not fully restrain an inner smile when he realized that he was concerned with perserving a woman's good name.

Just as he returned to Emily's side, the front door was flung open and Harper Brockinger himself stepped out. Cloud only briefly noted Dorothy quietly stepping out onto the veranda, but it was long enough to note the hungry look she cast his way, a look he coldly rebuffed, turning his full attention back to Harper and Emily. Outside of the surprise a man would naturally feel over seeing his baby sister all grown up, Harper looked only delighted and Cloud relaxed a little.

"Emily? That you?"

"Yes, I fear it is, Harper." She laughed a little shakily as he bounded down the steps to embrace her.

The next few minutes were decidedly hectic. Emily breathed a sigh of relief when they were finally seated in the parlour, Dorothy serving them tea. As carefully as she could, hoping not to stir bad memories in Thornton, who sat shyly at her side, Emily told the story of her journey. Cloud, who was sprawled on her other side on the settee, occasionally added a word.

"My God, Em. You're lucky to be alive. I can't thank you enough, Cloud. I know I owe you her life."

"Oh, I don't know." Cloud smiled faintly.

"Your sister's just bull-headed enough to have made it on her own."

"Your flattery leaves me speechless," Emily said softly, so that only Cloud heard her.

"So the boy returns with you, Mr. Ryder?" Dorothy asked coolly.

"I'm staying with Mama."

Emily barely managed to keep from spilling her tea when Thornton nearly leapt into her lap and eyed Dorothy belligerently. She thanked Cloud with a glance when he quickly relieved her of the cup. She put her arms around the child and suddenly knew for certain that she would not, could not, be separated from him. It was no longer just Thornton who saw her as his mother. She felt it too.

"Of course you are, love." She looked at her brother. "Thornton and I come as a pair. If that will cause some trouble . . ."

"None at all. We have plenty of room."

Although she pretended not to notice, Emily saw the look Harper sent his wife. She also found it easy to read, as easy as Dorothy's pinched expression. Harper clearly did not mind having the boy, but Dorothy just as clearly did. Emily was determined not to let that displeasure hurt Thornton in any way, even if it meant that she would have to leave.

As Harper and Cloud politely exchanged news, Emily covertly studied her sister-in-law. The woman had very light brown hair, fine features, a trim figure and lovely blue eyes. She should have been beautiful but there was, Emily mused, a tightness, a coldness, about Dorothy that stole her beauty. Dissatisfaction pinched the woman's face. Glancing around the expensively appointed parlour, Emily wondered what could dissatisfy the woman. She had everything most women would feel was vital to the good life and a handsome husband as well. Dorothy gave Emily an uneasy feeling, a warning that things would not be as rosy as she had imagined.

Shaking off that feeling, which was only enhanced by Dorothy's making no attempt to converse with her, Emily watched her brother. He looked the same, the years having simply honed his finely cut features. His sandy hair was still as thick and unruly as ever and his hazel eyes had only a few lines radiating from their corners. He looked like the Harper she remembered so fondly. She knew it would be a while before she found out how much else, if anything, had stayed the same.

When Cloud finally rose to leave, Emily hurried to follow him out. She noticed that Thornton stayed close to her even as she managed to get a moment's privacy with Cloud. Aware that Dorothy and Harper watched from the veranda, Emily maintained a stance of polite gratitude, but she knew her eyes revealed a lot more emotion and suspected that, despite her best efforts, they held a plea. She ruefully admitted that what she sought before he drove away was reassurance that he would come back.

"You be a good boy for your mother," Cloud ordered a sad-eyed Thornton as he affectionately ruffled the boy's hair.

"You'll come visit me?"

Watching Emily as he replied, Cloud said, "I sure will. I intend to see a lot of you and your mother." He stood up from where he had crouched before the boy. "I've got a few things I've got to sort out first. It'll take a week, probably two, then I'll be at the door."

Her heart fluttered with hope. "We'll be watching for you."

"Good. Then we'll have a serenade or two."

She had to force herself not to blush. He grinned as he said good-bye and climbed into the wagon. It was difficult not to stand there and watch him until he was out of sight, but she felt that might stir too many questions from her brother and Dorothy. The moment she returned to the house, she discovered that Dorothy needed no such action to stir suspicions. She was confronted by the woman in the hall before Harper had even finished closing the door.

"Just what happened between you two?" Dorothy asked straight out. "You and that libertine were alone together for weeks."

"Dorothy," Harper said warningly but his

wife ignored him.

"Hardly alone," Emily murmured. "We had Thornton and James Carlin with us."

"As if that would trouble that heathen. I want some answers. I want to know what sort of trouble I am facing. There will be talk, you know—talk about you and that man."

"The sort of talk that should not be spat out before a small child," Emily said quietly.

Dorothy sputtered with indignation and Harper took quick advantage of the break in his wife's assault. Collecting the bags Cloud had left in the hall, he ushered Emily and Thornton to their rooms. When he returned to the parlour, he found his wife angrily pacing the room. She turned on him and he sighed.

"You should have allowed me to question her."

"What good would that have done?"

"I would have gotten at the truth."

"If the truth is what you suspect it is—"

"Of course it is. The man's a rake, a womanizer. He was with your sister for weeks. I won't believe it if you try to claim that nothing happened."

"It doesn't matter what you believe. I repeat, if the truth is what you suspect, Emily sure as hell won't admit to it. No properly bred Boston lady would ever admit to doing anything scandalous. That rule's taught from the cradle. One avoids scandal at all costs."

"She can be as silent as the grave and people will still know what happened."

"Perhaps, nothing. It could have been innocent."

Dorothy gave him a contemptuous look. "You don't believe that any more than I do."

He said nothing but had to agree. Nothing could make him believe that. Emily had grown up into a lovely young woman. Cloud Ryder was not a man to resist such a temptation. Harper had also noticed the way the two had looked at each other. He had no doubt in his mind that they had been lovers. He would not, however, force Emily to admit to it. There was no point to that and nothing to be gained. He was not sure what Dorothy wanted, however.

"Are you expecting me to demand satisfaction or something of the like?"

"Do be sensible, Harper. I certainly don't want you challenging that uncivilized man, and I don't want you demanding that he marry Emily. Think, Harper. Remember the reason you asked Emily out here? What happens to that plan now? You don't think Chilton will remain ignorant of what's happened, do you? It'll be all over town in hours. He probably won't want the silly girl now."

Harper frowned and, after a moment's thought, said quietly, "Actually, I think he just might want her all the more." He sighed. "Yes, I think he'll find it very interesting, especially if Cloud Ryder continues to show an interest in Emily."

Emily sighed and collapsed on the bed once she reached her room. Thornton did not want to stay, and she had been hard pressed to quiet his protests, especially since she could understand his reluctance. Dorothy had made her distaste for the child all too apparent. Thornton did not really believe her assurances that that would change once Dorothy got to know him. Neither, Emily admitted sadly, did she.

As the day dragged on, Emily's spirits plunged. No more mention was made about what may or may not have happened between her and Cloud on the journey, but she knew that both Harper and Dorothy had not decided in favor of her innocence. For a moment she was sorely tempted to tell them the whole truth, but common sense intervened. It would do none of them any good and could even cause Cloud some difficulty, which was the last thing she wanted. She realized that Harper's presence had been the only reason for Dorothy's forbearance when the woman caught her alone on the stairs for a moment as they all retired for the night.

"You think you've managed to slip through all this with no trouble and no need for repentence, don't you?"

"Perhaps, Dorothy, I have no need to be repentent." Emily felt a strong urge to strike the woman, but that boded ill for the harmonious relationship she still hoped to establish.

"Nonsense. You spent weeks with that man. He is notorious."

"So, of course, I must be as well."

Dorothy ignored that. "Harper and I intend to help you overcome this scandal."

"How kind of you."

"You'll hear the talk soon and see the looks. Don't think that man will do anything to help you. You've seen the last of him."

"You're sure of that, are you?"

"Quite sure and you're a foolish little girl if you think otherwise. Cloud Ryder has used and cast aside more women than anyone cares to count. Don't get to thinking that some little naive miss from Boston can change that. You'd better look elsewhere and start soon."

Emily tried very hard not to heed Dorothy's words. She wanted to believe in Cloud. He had said he would come back and, although she did not want to put all of her hopes on that, she did not want to doubt him.

As the days began to add up, she found her faith in Cloud Ryder harder and harder to maintain. It did not really surprise her that there was no word from him, but she heartily wished he would send some. Even the briefest of messages would have helped. Instead she sat waiting without sight or word from him to bolster her wavering confidence in his return, a confidence Dorothy continually undermined with her seemingly endless reminders of Cloud's notoriety and faithlessness concerning women.

Finding a friend helped her a little. Walking through town one evening, Emily came upon a man harassing a thin, redheaded girl who looked hardly old enough to be attracting male attention. Marching into the fray, Emily managed to extract the girl from her difficulty and they both fled. Giorsal MacGregor proved a diversion Emily sorely needed, even though the girl refused to go near Dorothy. Emily made an evening stroll a habit so that she could meet Giorsal and the two of them could pass a few hours in idle chatter. Emily considered it the best of ways to end what were becoming interminably long days.

Two weeks later, Cloud reined in before Harper's and tried to quell an unaccustomed nervousness. He had not quite finished his plans but had convinced himself that he was ready enough. It was a need to see Emily that drove him and he knew it. Despite wanting a more stable and attractive future to lay out before her, he could no longer wait to see her.

Dismounting and lightly securing his

horse, he struggled to pull together his suddenly tattered confidence. That struggle amused him a little even as it irritated and worried him. Confidence with women was not something he had ever had much trouble with before.

When Dorothy answered his rap on the door, he was less than pleased. The woman went out of her way to touch him as she drew him into the front hall. Even if he had not been involved with Emily, Cloud knew he would never have returned the woman's interest. Dorothy Brockinger was one of those women he avoided like the plague—a manipulative, greedy, and haughty woman whom no one and nothing could ever make happy.

"I've come to see Em." He found it hard to be polite but, for Emily's sake, was determined to do his best.

"She has gone up to rest after church. Perhaps if you come back later."

"She's expecting me."

"Of course. I'll go tell her you are here."

He smiled crookedly as she walked up the stairs. For a haughty woman who had pushed herself to the top of what little society there was in town, she had a very come-hither sway. He wondered idly if Harper knew how easily he could find himself cuckolded, then turned his thoughts to what he would say to Emily.

"Psst! Uncle Cloud? It's me." Thornton

slipped into the hall from the parlour, his gaze shifting and narrowed as he looked around.

"Hello, Thornton. Something wrong?" Cloud was suddenly aware of the boy's somewhat sneaky air as he crouched before the boy.

"Nope. I don't want *her* to see me."

"Dorothy? Mrs. Brockinger?"

"Yeah. Her don't like me."

Cloud did not doubt the boy's opinion for a moment. "Does she give you trouble, Thornton? Is she mean?"

"Nope. Just don't like me round. Always telling me to go 'way. Are you here to take us away from here?"

Before he could reply, the boy slipped away. As he stood up, Cloud was not surprised to see Dorothy returning. He was troubled by the way Thornton had acted, but those concerns were pushed to the background when he saw that Dorothy had returned alone.

"Where's Em?" The tension he felt suddenly knotting his insides made his voice curt.

"Oh, my, I don't know what to say." Dorothy's hand fluttered nervously to her throat as she eyed him warily.

"Did you tell her I wanted to see her?"

"Yes, yes I did. She's very tired and I suspect it has made her ill-tempered."

"What did she say?" he demanded coldly,

feeling his whole body tense as if readying for a blow.

"I told her you were here to see her," Dorothy replied with strained reluctance, "and she said she doesn't want to see you. She said—well, she said that what happened between the two of you was best forgotten."

Shock silenced Cloud for several minutes. Then his eyes turned cold, making Dorothy shiver slightly. "Forgotten it is," he said flatly and, sharply turning, strode out of the house.

"What was that all about?"

Dorothy, who had been watching Cloud ride away, squeaked in surprise and turned to look at her husband. "You frightened me." She shut the door, then started into the parlour. "How long have you been lurking out of sight?" she asked crossly as he finished descending the stairs and followed her.

"I saw you standing in the upstairs hall counting to twenty and decided you were acting strange enough to warrant a closer look. What did Cloud Ryder want?"

"To see Emily."

"And you didn't even tell her he was here."

"No, and you won't either." Even though it was still early on a Sunday, Dorothy decided she wanted a drink and, ignoring Harper's glance of disapproval, poured herself one. "Want one, dear?"

"No. I want to know what plot you're

hatching now."

"No plot except the one we hatched together when we invited your sister here. Chilton and the money, remember?"

"Of course I remember. It's not easy to forget a debt that big. What does that have to do with lying to that man, to Emily?"

"Think, Harper, for God's sake." She sat down on the settee and wondered crossly what Emily possessed that drew a man like Cloud to the door, hat in hand, while she had never gained even the slightest spark of interest. "She's been moping around here watching for him. Chilton can't stir a spark of interest in her, and it's because of that man."

Harper doubted that was the only reason but declined to say so. "So you neatly get rid of Cloud Ryder."

"Of course. Would you rather I let him start sniffing around your sister again? That it would ruin any bargain with Chilton goes without saying. To my surprise, you were right. The man did seem even more interested in Emily after he heard about Ryder. However, he won't be pleased if we allow Ryder to keep coming around the girl. Then there is the scandal that would arise if we let her associate with that half-breed rogue. I certainly don't want to hear it or suffer it, thank you very much."

She leaned forward. "I won't let that half-breed ruin what chance we've managed to grasp to pull us out of the hole we're in, nor will I let your sister's folly do it. He didn't come, he's never come, and that's that. Let her think herself deserted. It's the only way to save ourselves."

After a moment's hesitation, while rebellion stirred faintly in his breast, Harper nodded.

Chapter Thirteen

"That's the Peterson home. My bank holds their mortgage as well."

Emily turned away from the man driving the buggy and rolled her eyes. Thomas Chilton clearly considered any building mortgaged to him a point of interest. He was the sort of man, she mused, that gave bankers a bad name. She wished she had not agreed to a drive before dinner. It had been a mistake to think the man would improve with time. She gave a little start when she realized he was still talking to her.

"I was pleased when I heard you intended to join our growing community."

"Thank you, Mr. Chilton."

"Yes, we need women like you in Lockridge. Women of breeding. Women who know what's proper and have learned all those social refinements that are so valuable to a town."

What a snob, she thought but murmured a polite response.

"Coming from Philadelphia myself, I sorely miss that gentility. I began to think it unattainable out here. Now I can see there is hope. Yes, with women like you and Dorothy here, things certainly look brighter for Lockridge."

"I'm glad you think so, Mr. Chilton." She frowned when he stopped the buggy at a somewhat deserted spot a short distance from Harper's house. "Is something wrong?"

"No. I felt it would be nice to have a moment or two alone."

"I'm not sure that's proper, Mr. Chilton." She thought she saw annoyance flicker through his eyes, but it came and went too quickly for her to be sure.

"I don't believe you understand what a desert for the senses and the mind Lockridge has been." He took her hand in his.

Emily frowned as he sidled closer and she subtly but fruitlessly tried to free her hand from his. "I'm sorry to hear that, Mr. Chilton."

"From the moment I saw your picture and Harper told me about you, I knew I had to meet you. There isn't a woman here suitable for a man in my position. No one with the proper upbringing and background.

A man like me needs a genteel lady he is not ashamed to introduce to his business associates, one he can take into the finest homes, who can even help him to get there."

Emily decided she did not like the trend of this conversation at all, nor how close he was pressing to her. "Mr. Chilton . . ." She tightened her grip on her parasol.

"A woman like you can only help a man climb that ladder to success."

He put his hand on her knee and squeezed slightly. Even as Emily stared at it, wondering how his touch could feel cold through several layers of dress and petticoat, he inched his hand up from her knee. Without another moment's hesitation, she brought her parasol down squarely on his head, and his curse nearly drowned out the sound of the parasol splintering. While he clutched his head and checked for signs of blood she jumped out of the carriage and ran for Harper's house. Her pace slowed when she realized he was not giving chase. Once back in the house, she hurried up to her room before Dorothy could ask after Chilton. She heartily wished the man would be too embarrassed to come to dinner, but she doubted it.

Letting go the yawn she had stifled for the entire evening, Emily prepared herself for the lecture she was sure was coming. She had not been very civil to Mr. Chilton. The man could not help it if he reminded her of a weasel and was an excruciating bore. She was also still annoyed, even disturbed, over the incident in the buggy. Emily just wished she could shake the feeling that there was a plot afoot. Thomas Chilton's actions during the buggy ride only enhanced that feeling.

It was a feeling that had been with her almost since her arrival three weeks ago. Harper was not as she had remembered him, something she attributed to his narrow-eyed, tight-lipped wife. Even so, he was her brother and it seemed disloyal to think that he intended something underhanded.

On the other hand, Dorothy was quite capable of plots. Emily knew it was not her imagination that told her that Harper's wife disliked her. She was sure Dorothy had not extended the slim hospitality of her home without good reason. Emily just wished that she could figure out what that reason was.

She sighed as she wondered if her worrying about plots was simply a distraction clung to in order to not think about Cloud. He had said he would come back, that he wanted to see her again, yet three long weeks had gone by. Emily did not really think that his "few items" should take so long. She could not help but feel that, once away from her, he had decided to stay away, and that hurt her deeply.

Just as she had tried not to, she had hoped. She had read a promise of continuity in his passion during their last night together that had not been there before. With her body had gone her heart, and now she was paying for her lack of good sense. A man like him had no use for love and the ties that went with it.

The problem was that she did, especially now that she grew more certain with each passing day that his child grew inside of her. From what little she knew, the signs were right. Soon she would have to speak to her friend Giorsal, for if it was not a child thickening her waistline and stopping her flow, then she was in sore need of a skilled doctor. She was, however, fairly certain it was a baby, for tumors could not quicken and move within a woman's womb with promising life.

"Look at her mooning over that damned half-breed Ryder."

Emily winced as Dorothy's strident voice greeted on her ears. "He is only one-fourth Indian."

"Oh, I beg your pardon," Dorothy shrilled sarcastically. "Little that matters. Indian's Indian. The man's no good anyhow. Doesn't even have a sod hut on his land."

"Dotty, honey, Cloud Ryder isn't at issue here," Harper said as he wearily took a seat.

"Isn't he? If she weren't so besotted by the villain she'd be nicer to Thomas."

"I don't think so," Emily said coolly. "The man is a bore."

"A bore is he? Well, I suggest you learn to smile even if it hurts."

"Dotty, I think this isn't the right time,"